MANGA MYSTERIES

MATH

#6

THE FISHY FOUNTAIN

A Mystery with Multiplication and Division

by Melinda Thielbar

illustrated by Yali Lin

GRAPHIC UNIVERSE™ • MINNEAPOLIS • NEW YORK

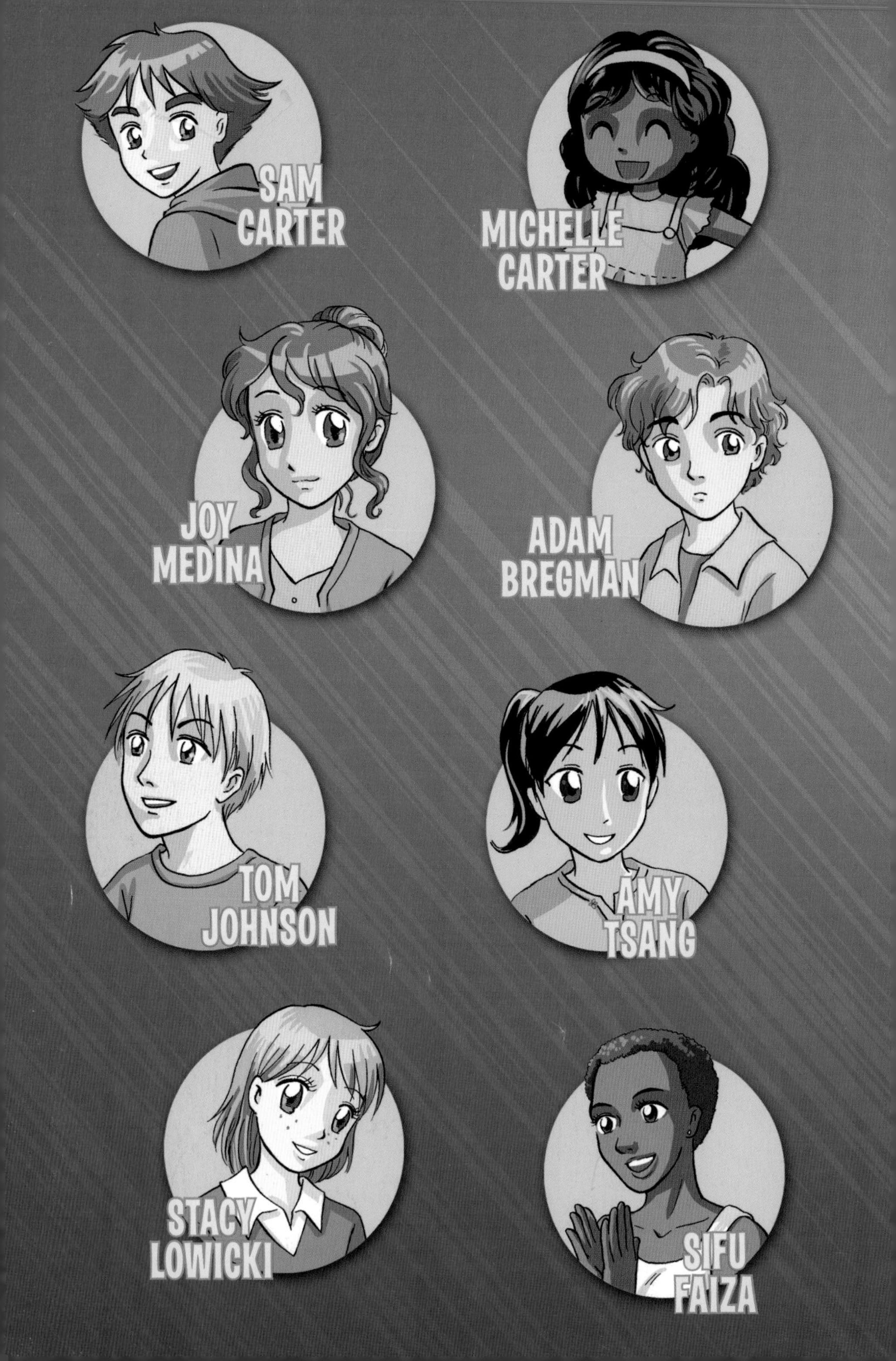
SAM CARTER
MICHELLE CARTER
JOY MEDINA
ADAM BREGMAN
TOM JOHNSON
AMY TSANG
STACY LOWICKI
SIFU FAIZA

STACY'S MOM

MR. HALLORAN

MR. FELS

What is multiplication? Multiplication is a way to combine equal groups. It is like adding the same number over and over. 3 times 2 is the same as adding 2 three times:

$$2 + 2 + 2 = 6 \qquad 3 \times 2 = 6$$

The numbers being multiplied are called **factors.** The answer is called the **product.**

What is division? Division is the opposite of multiplication. Division separates an amount into smaller equal groups, to find the number of groups or the number in each group. For example, if there are 12 carrots and 4 people, each person gets 3 carrots, or: $12 \div 4 = 3$

If there are 6 socks and there are 2 socks in a pair, there can be 3 pairs of socks, or: $6 \div 2 = 3$

The number being divided is the **dividend.** The number that divides it is the **divisor.** The answer is the **quotient.**

Story by Melinda Thielbar
Pencils and inks by Yali Lin
Coloring by Jenn Manley Lee
Lettering by Zack Giallongo

Graphic Universe™
A division of Lerner Publishing Group, Inc.
241 First Avenue North
Minneapolis, MN 55401 U.S.A.

Website address: www.lernerbooks.com

Library of Congress Cataloging-in-Publication Data

Thielbar, Melinda.
    The fishy fountain : a mystery with multiplication and division / by Melinda Thielbar ; illustrated by Yali Lin.
        p. cm. — (Manga math mysteries ; #6)
        Summary: After a prank is pulled putting dangerous chemicals in the fountain at Stacy's new science magnet school, four friends from Sifu Faiza's Kung Fu School use multiplication and division to help figure out who did it and how.
        ISBN: 978-0-7613-4908-2 (lib. bdg. : alk. paper)
        1. Graphic novels. [1. Graphic novels. 2. Mystery and detective stories. 3. Mathematics—Fiction. 4. Schools—Fiction.] I. Lin, Yali, ill. II. Title.
    PZ7.7.T48Fi 2011
    741.5'973—dc22   2010002426

Manufactured in the United States of America
1 – DP – 7/15/10

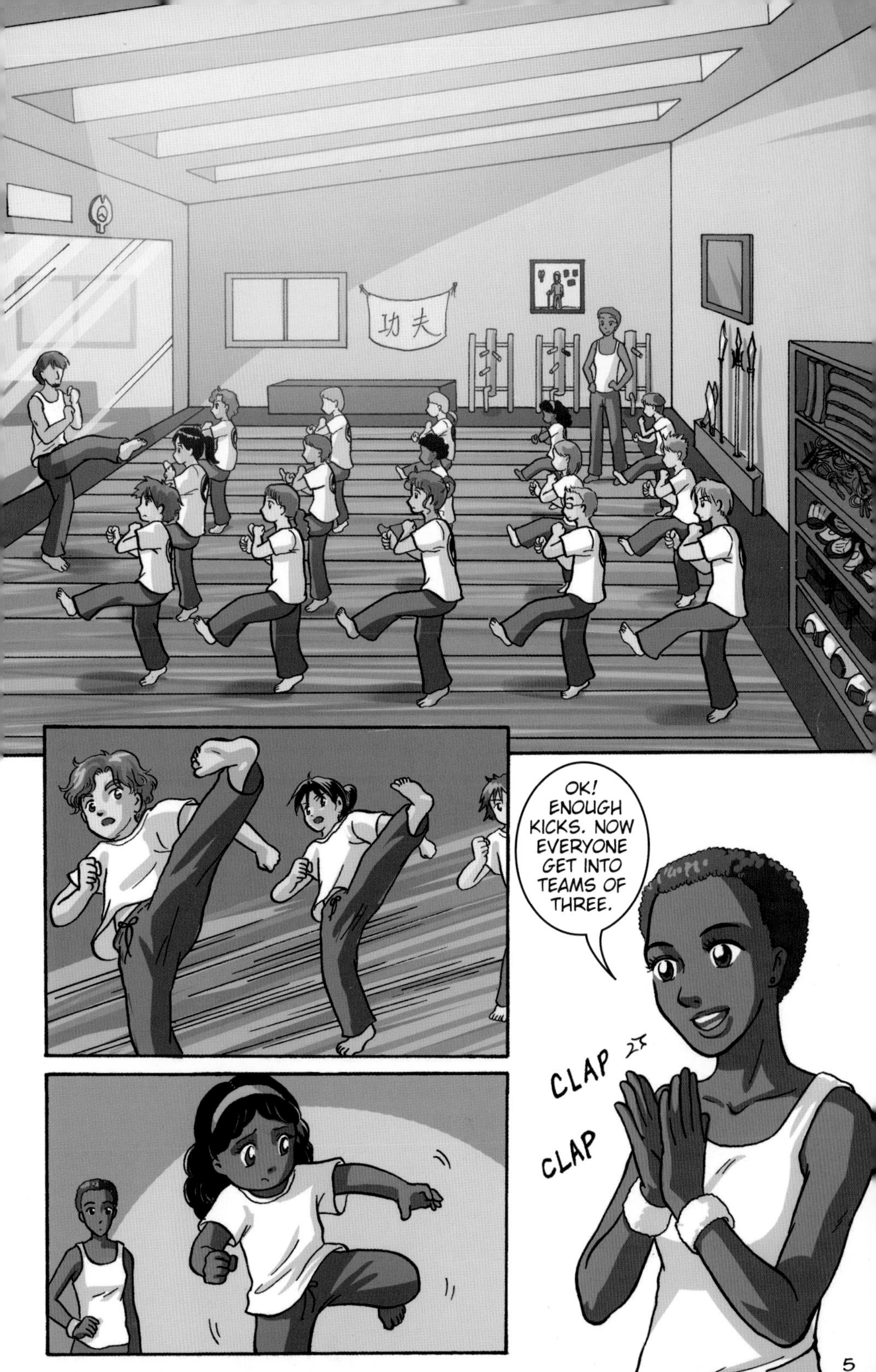
功夫
OK! ENOUGH KICKS. NOW EVERYONE GET INTO TEAMS OF THREE.
CLAP
CLAP

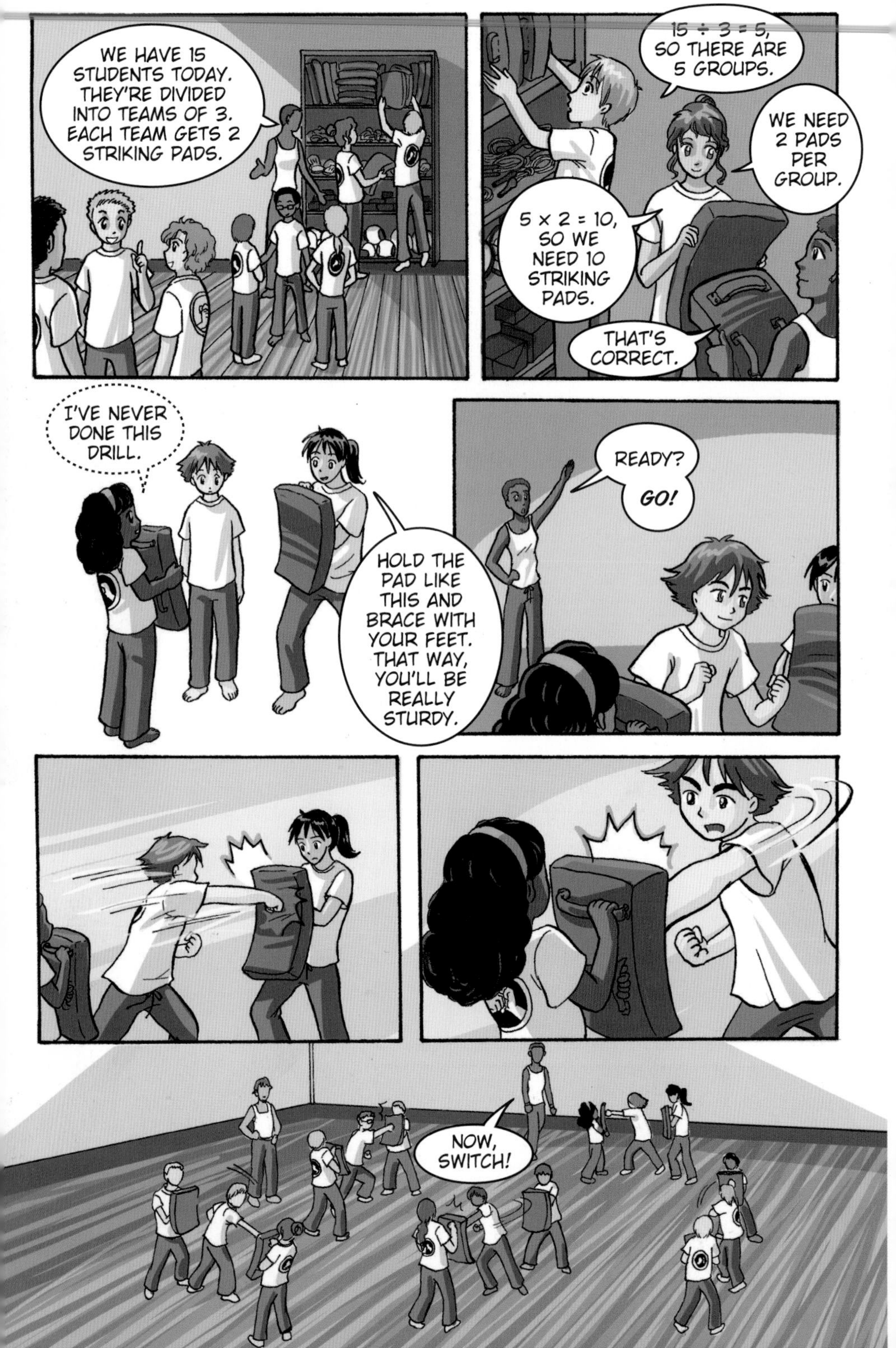
WE HAVE 15 STUDENTS TODAY. THEY'RE DIVIDED INTO TEAMS OF 3. EACH TEAM GETS 2 STRIKING PADS.
15 ÷ 3 = 5, SO THERE ARE 5 GROUPS.
WE NEED 2 PADS PER GROUP.
5 x 2 = 10, SO WE NEED 10 STRIKING PADS.
THAT'S CORRECT.
I'VE NEVER DONE THIS DRILL.
HOLD THE PAD LIKE THIS AND BRACE WITH YOUR FEET. THAT WAY, YOU'LL BE REALLY STURDY.
READY?
GO!
NOW, SWITCH!

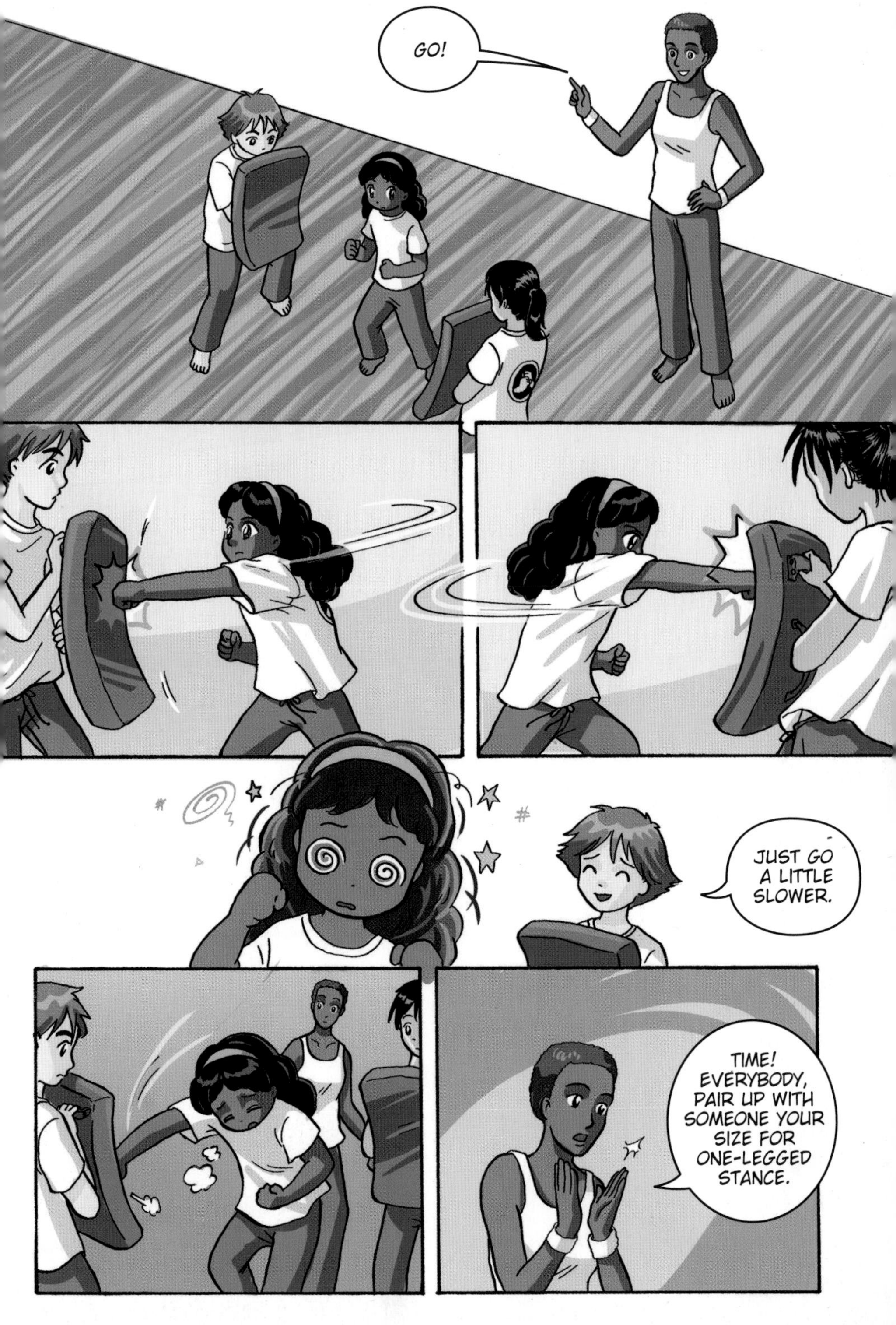
GO!
JUST GO A LITTLE SLOWER.
TIME! EVERYBODY, PAIR UP WITH SOMEONE YOUR SIZE FOR ONE-LEGGED STANCE.

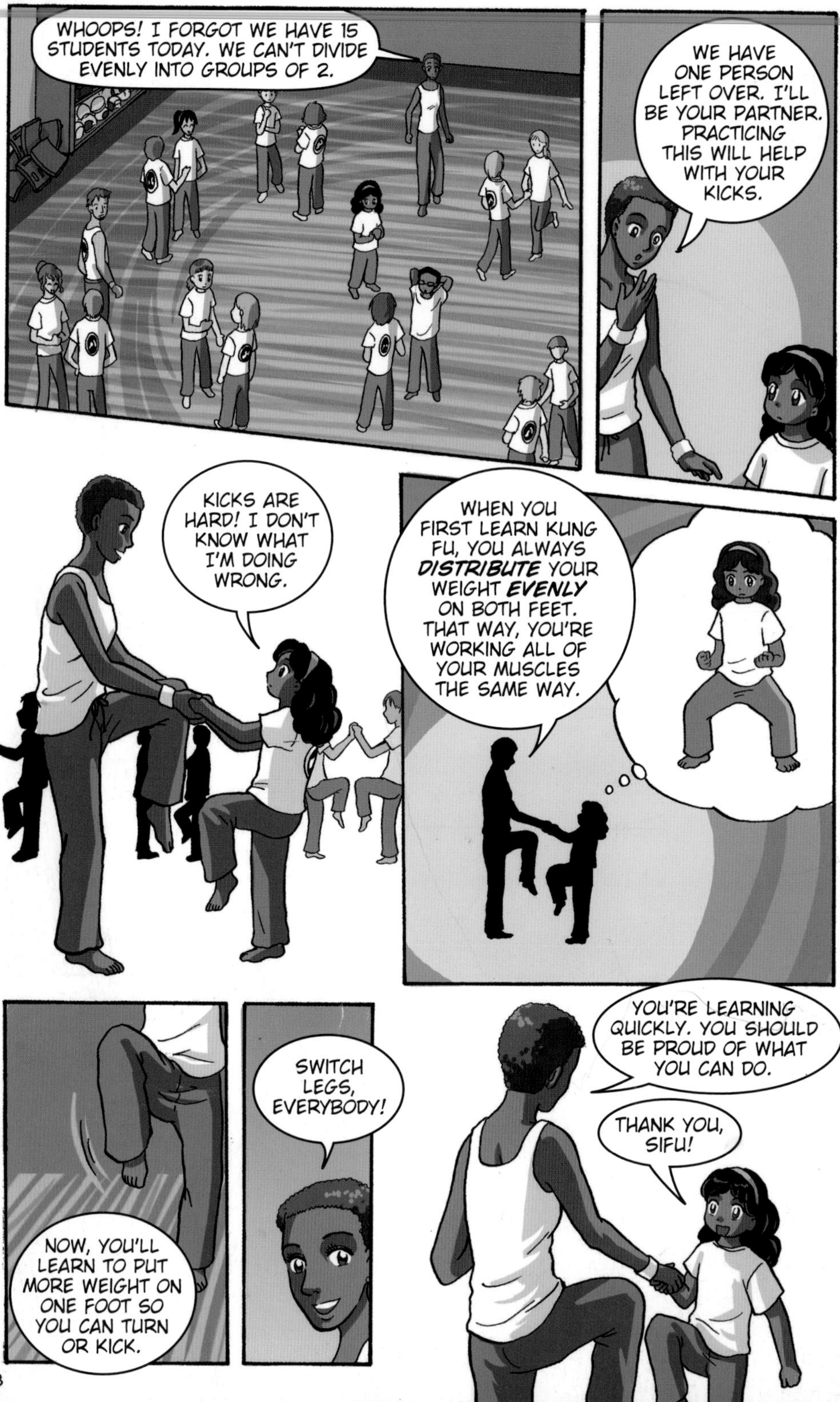

WHOOPS! I FORGOT WE HAVE 15 STUDENTS TODAY. WE CAN'T DIVIDE EVENLY INTO GROUPS OF 2.
WE HAVE ONE PERSON LEFT OVER. I'LL BE YOUR PARTNER. PRACTICING THIS WILL HELP WITH YOUR KICKS.
KICKS ARE HARD! I DON'T KNOW WHAT I'M DOING WRONG.
WHEN YOU FIRST LEARN KUNG FU, YOU ALWAYS ***DISTRIBUTE*** YOUR WEIGHT ***EVENLY*** ON BOTH FEET. THAT WAY, YOU'RE WORKING ALL OF YOUR MUSCLES THE SAME WAY.
NOW, YOU'LL LEARN TO PUT MORE WEIGHT ON ONE FOOT SO YOU CAN TURN OR KICK.
SWITCH LEGS, EVERYBODY!
YOU'RE LEARNING QUICKLY. YOU SHOULD BE PROUD OF WHAT YOU CAN DO.
THANK YOU, SIFU!

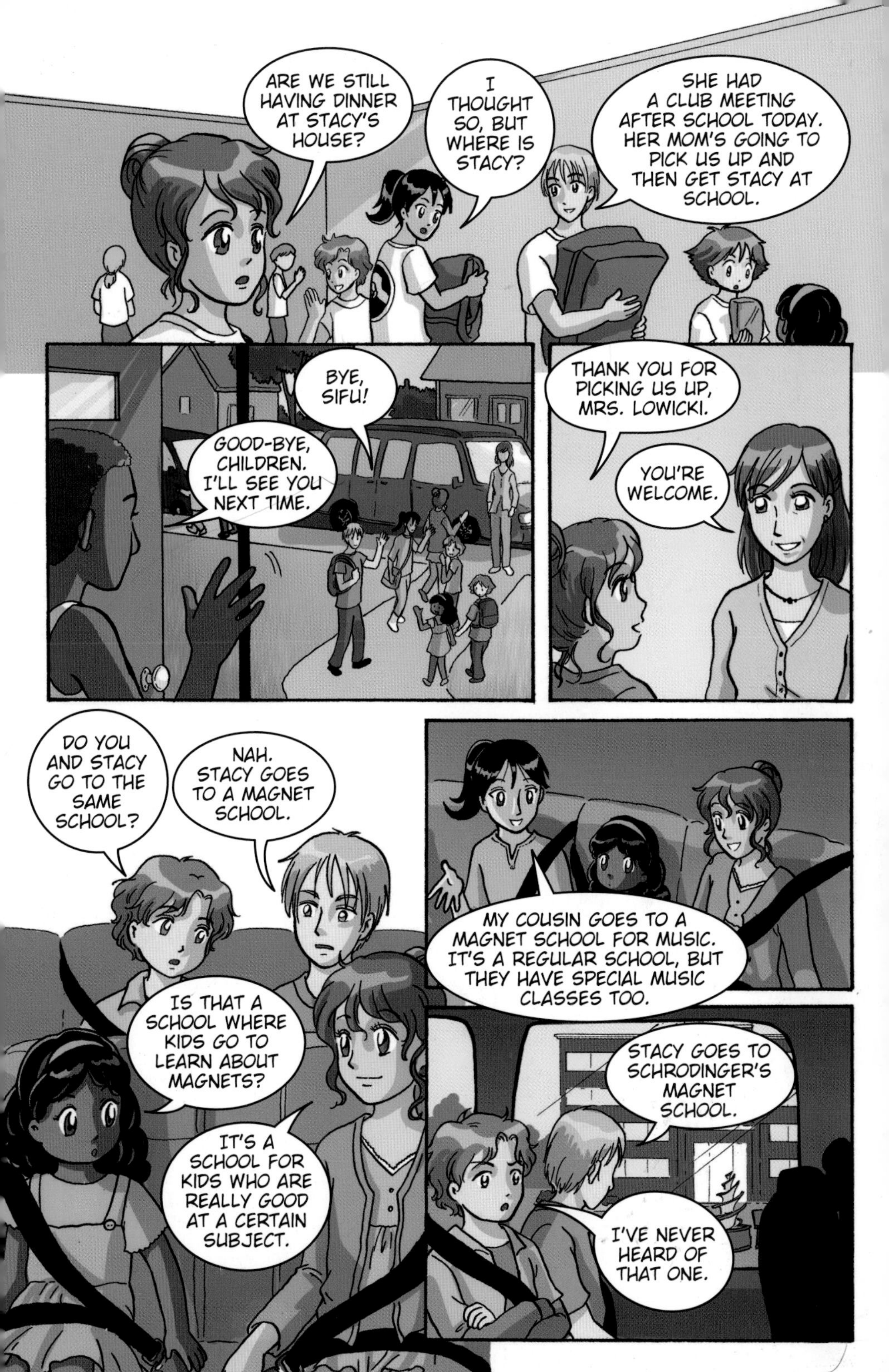
ARE WE STILL HAVING DINNER AT STACY'S HOUSE?
I THOUGHT SO, BUT WHERE IS STACY?
SHE HAD A CLUB MEETING AFTER SCHOOL TODAY. HER MOM'S GOING TO PICK US UP AND THEN GET STACY AT SCHOOL.
BYE, SIFU!
GOOD-BYE, CHILDREN. I'LL SEE YOU NEXT TIME.
THANK YOU FOR PICKING US UP, MRS. LOWICKI.
YOU'RE WELCOME.
DO YOU AND STACY GO TO THE SAME SCHOOL?
NAH. STACY GOES TO A MAGNET SCHOOL.
IS THAT A SCHOOL WHERE KIDS GO TO LEARN ABOUT MAGNETS?
IT'S A SCHOOL FOR KIDS WHO ARE REALLY GOOD AT A CERTAIN SUBJECT.
MY COUSIN GOES TO A MAGNET SCHOOL FOR MUSIC. IT'S A REGULAR SCHOOL, BUT THEY HAVE SPECIAL MUSIC CLASSES TOO.
STACY GOES TO SCHRODINGER'S MAGNET SCHOOL.
I'VE NEVER HEARD OF THAT ONE.

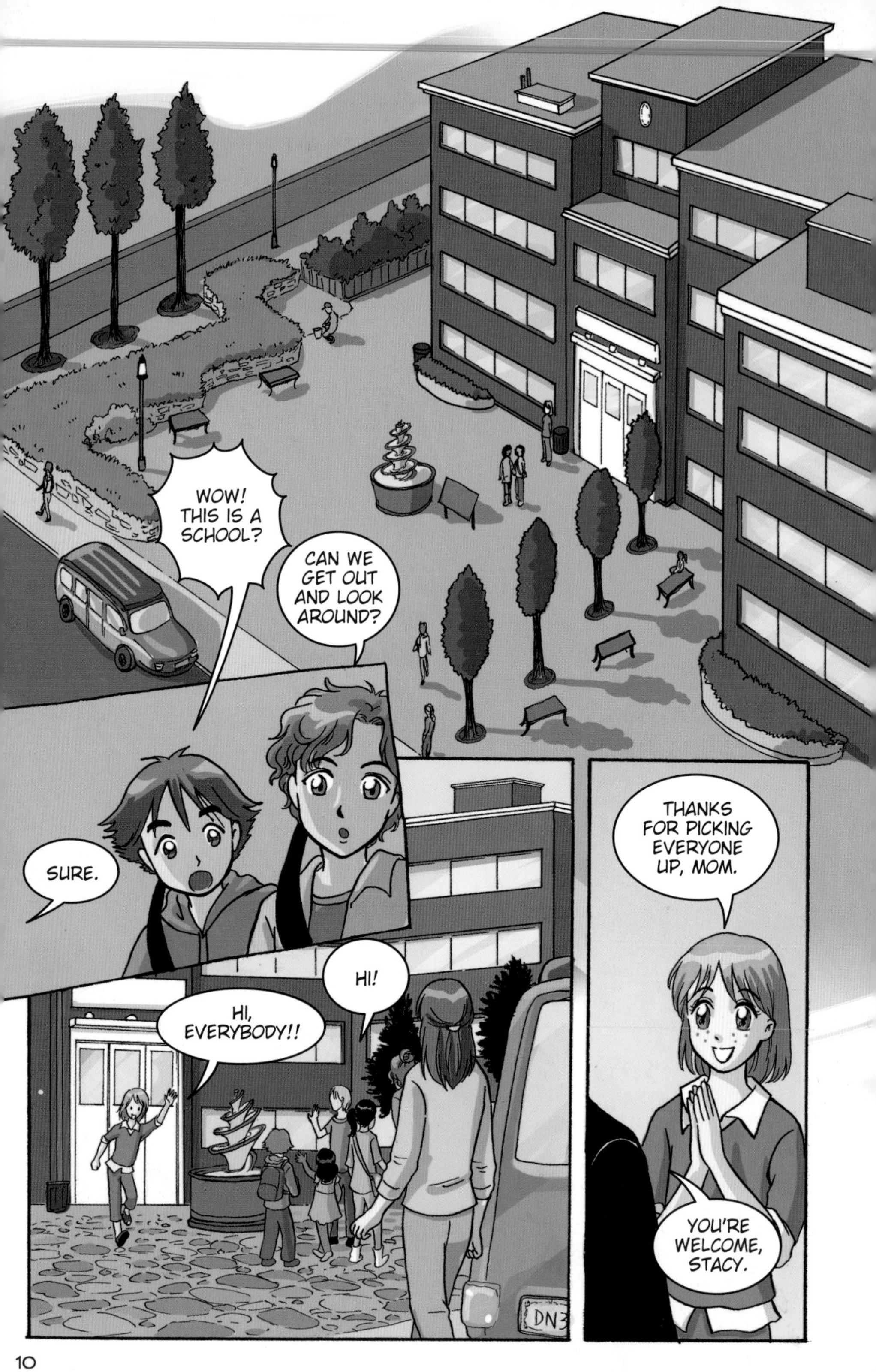
WOW! THIS IS A SCHOOL?
CAN WE GET OUT AND LOOK AROUND?
SURE.
HI, EVERYBODY!!
HI!
DN3
THANKS FOR PICKING EVERYONE UP, MOM.
YOU'RE WELCOME, STACY.

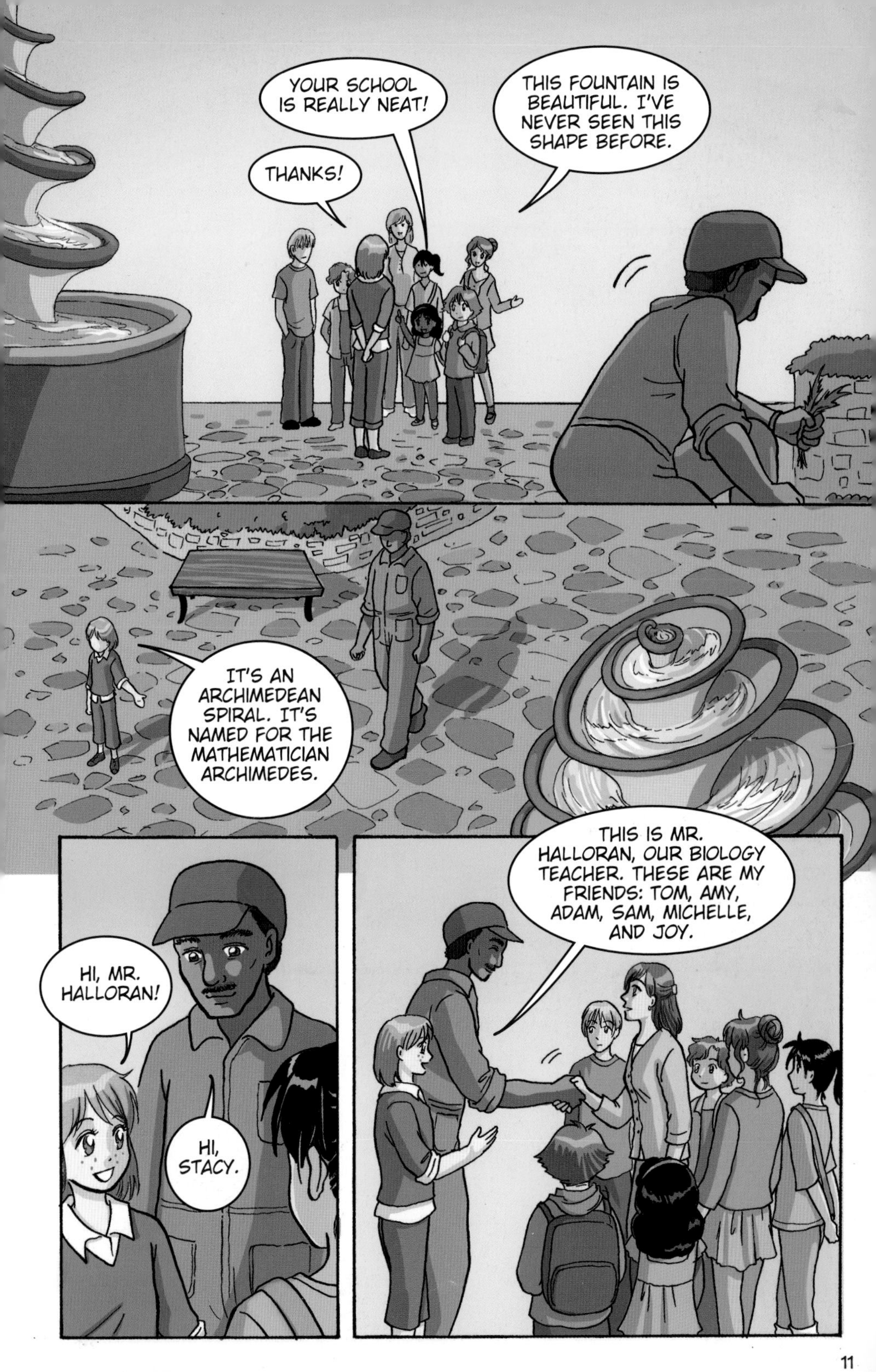
YOUR SCHOOL IS REALLY NEAT!
THANKS!
THIS FOUNTAIN IS BEAUTIFUL. I'VE NEVER SEEN THIS SHAPE BEFORE.
IT'S AN ARCHIMEDEAN SPIRAL. IT'S NAMED FOR THE MATHEMATICIAN ARCHIMEDES.
HI, MR. HALLORAN!
HI, STACY.
THIS IS MR. HALLORAN, OUR BIOLOGY TEACHER. THESE ARE MY FRIENDS: TOM, AMY, ADAM, SAM, MICHELLE, AND JOY.

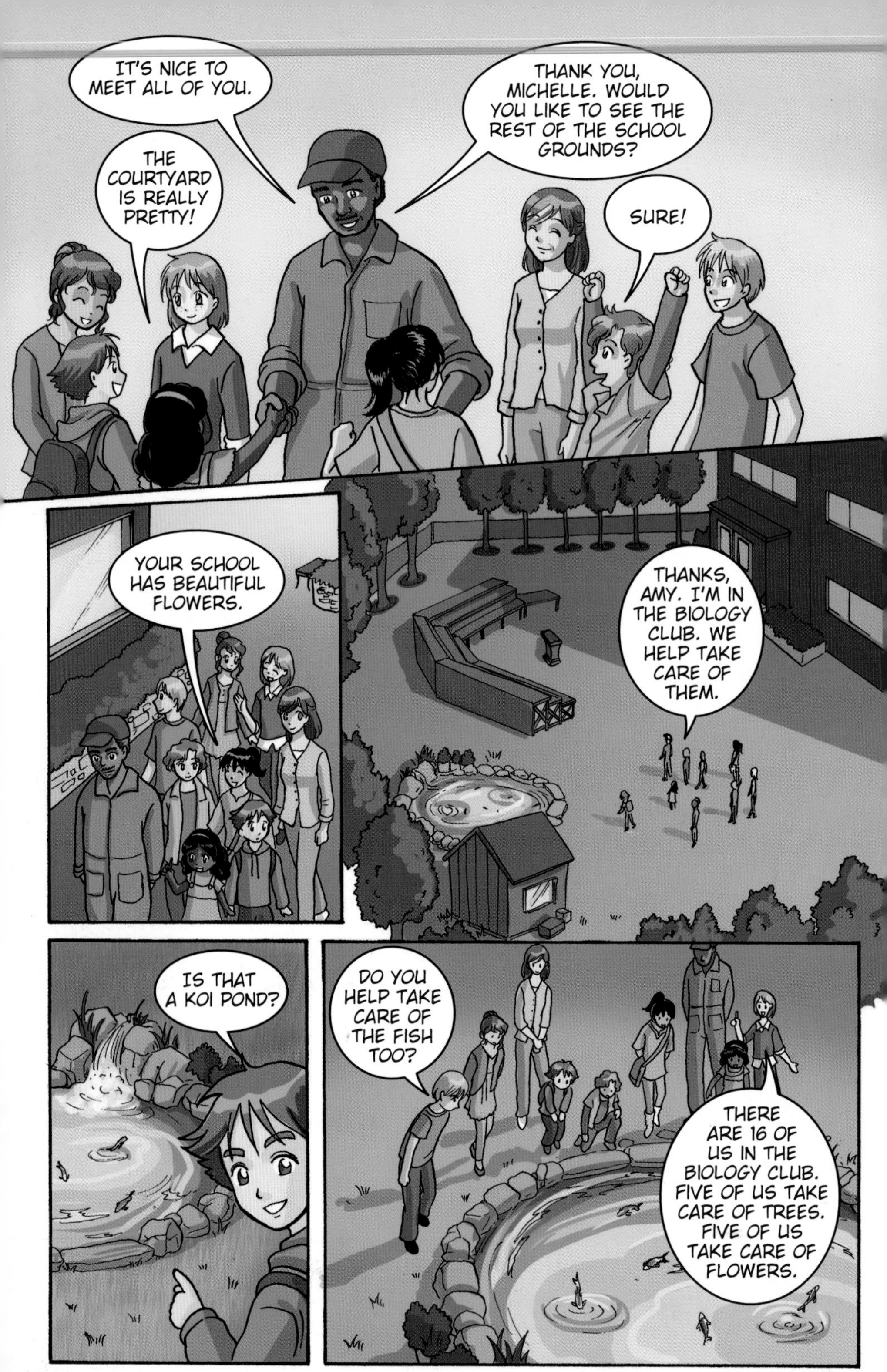
IT'S NICE TO MEET ALL OF YOU.
THE COURTYARD IS REALLY PRETTY!
THANK YOU, MICHELLE. WOULD YOU LIKE TO SEE THE REST OF THE SCHOOL GROUNDS?
SURE!
YOUR SCHOOL HAS BEAUTIFUL FLOWERS.
THANKS, AMY. I'M IN THE BIOLOGY CLUB. WE HELP TAKE CARE OF THEM.
IS THAT A KOI POND?
DO YOU HELP TAKE CARE OF THE FISH TOO?
THERE ARE 16 OF US IN THE BIOLOGY CLUB. FIVE OF US TAKE CARE OF TREES. FIVE OF US TAKE CARE OF FLOWERS.

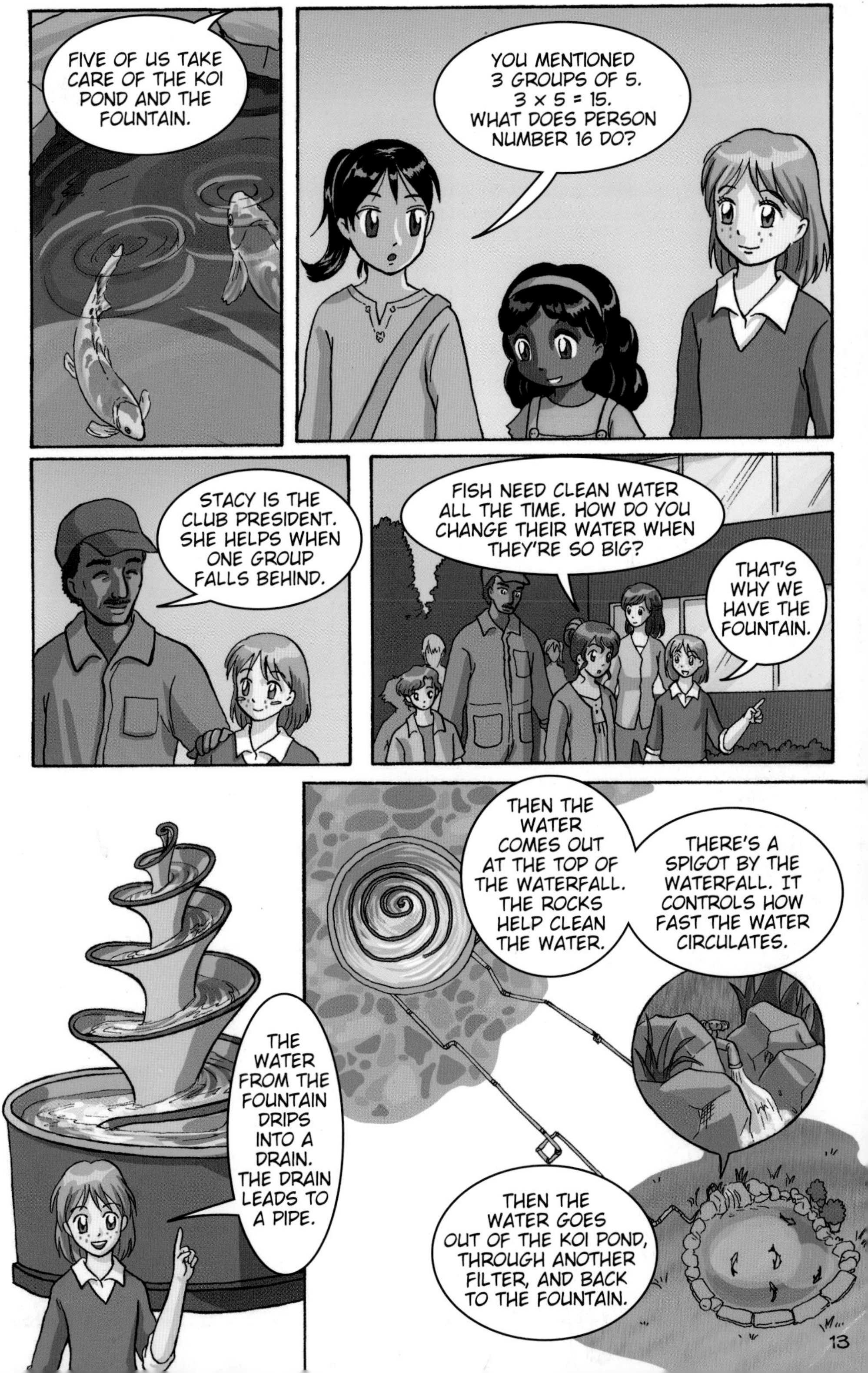

FIVE OF US TAKE CARE OF THE KOI POND AND THE FOUNTAIN.
YOU MENTIONED 3 GROUPS OF 5. 3 x 5 = 15. WHAT DOES PERSON NUMBER 16 DO?
STACY IS THE CLUB PRESIDENT. SHE HELPS WHEN ONE GROUP FALLS BEHIND.
FISH NEED CLEAN WATER ALL THE TIME. HOW DO YOU CHANGE THEIR WATER WHEN THEY'RE SO BIG?
THAT'S WHY WE HAVE THE FOUNTAIN.
THE WATER FROM THE FOUNTAIN DRIPS INTO A DRAIN. THE DRAIN LEADS TO A PIPE.
THEN THE WATER COMES OUT AT THE TOP OF THE WATERFALL. THE ROCKS HELP CLEAN THE WATER.
THERE'S A SPIGOT BY THE WATERFALL. IT CONTROLS HOW FAST THE WATER CIRCULATES.
THEN THE WATER GOES OUT OF THE KOI POND, THROUGH ANOTHER FILTER, AND BACK TO THE FOUNTAIN.

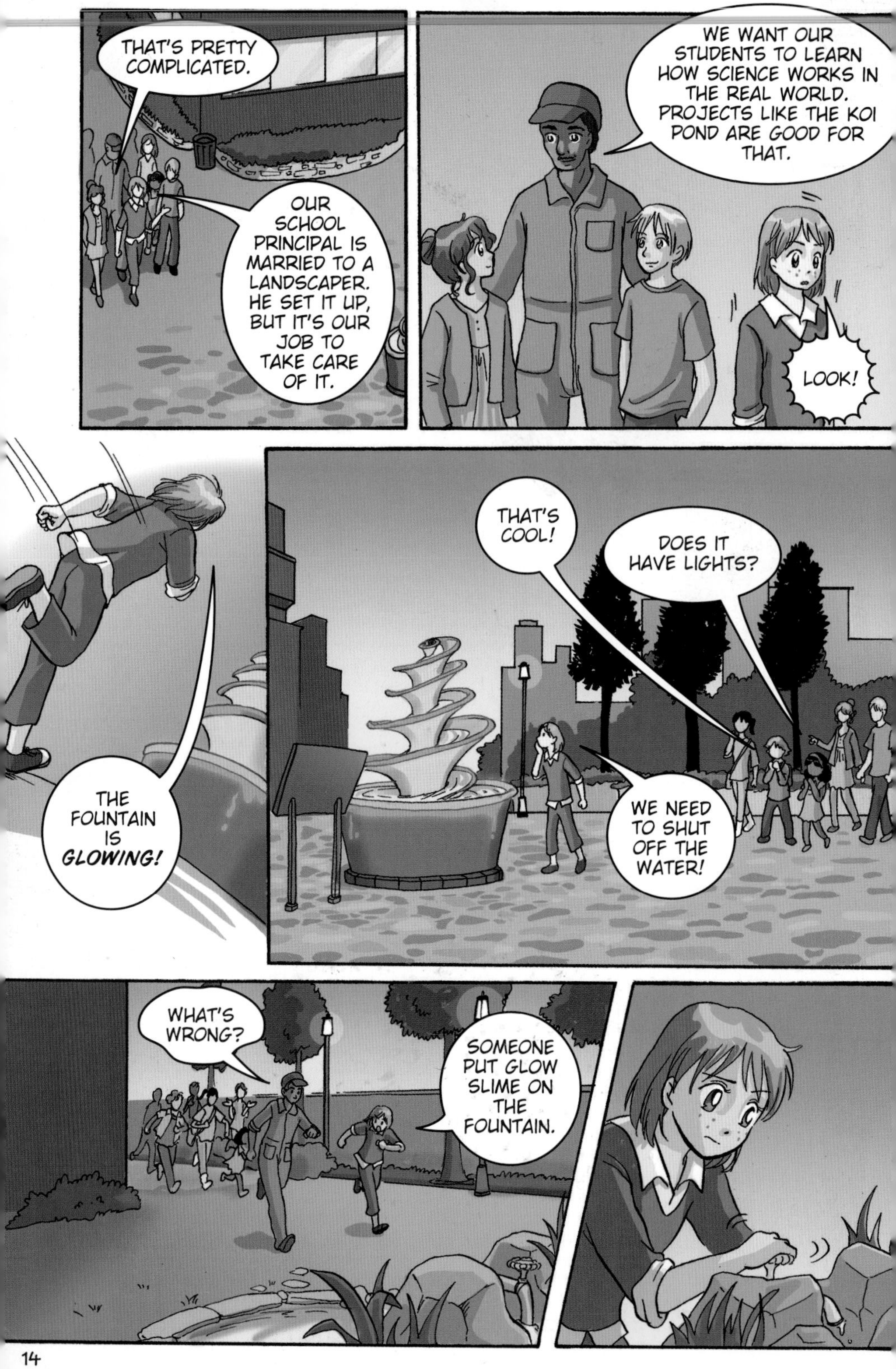
THAT'S PRETTY COMPLICATED.
OUR SCHOOL PRINCIPAL IS MARRIED TO A LANDSCAPER. HE SET IT UP, BUT IT'S OUR JOB TO TAKE CARE OF IT.
WE WANT OUR STUDENTS TO LEARN HOW SCIENCE WORKS IN THE REAL WORLD. PROJECTS LIKE THE KOI POND ARE GOOD FOR THAT.
LOOK!
THE FOUNTAIN IS *GLOWING!*
THAT'S COOL!
DOES IT HAVE LIGHTS?
WE NEED TO SHUT OFF THE WATER!
WHAT'S WRONG?
SOMEONE PUT GLOW SLIME ON THE FOUNTAIN.

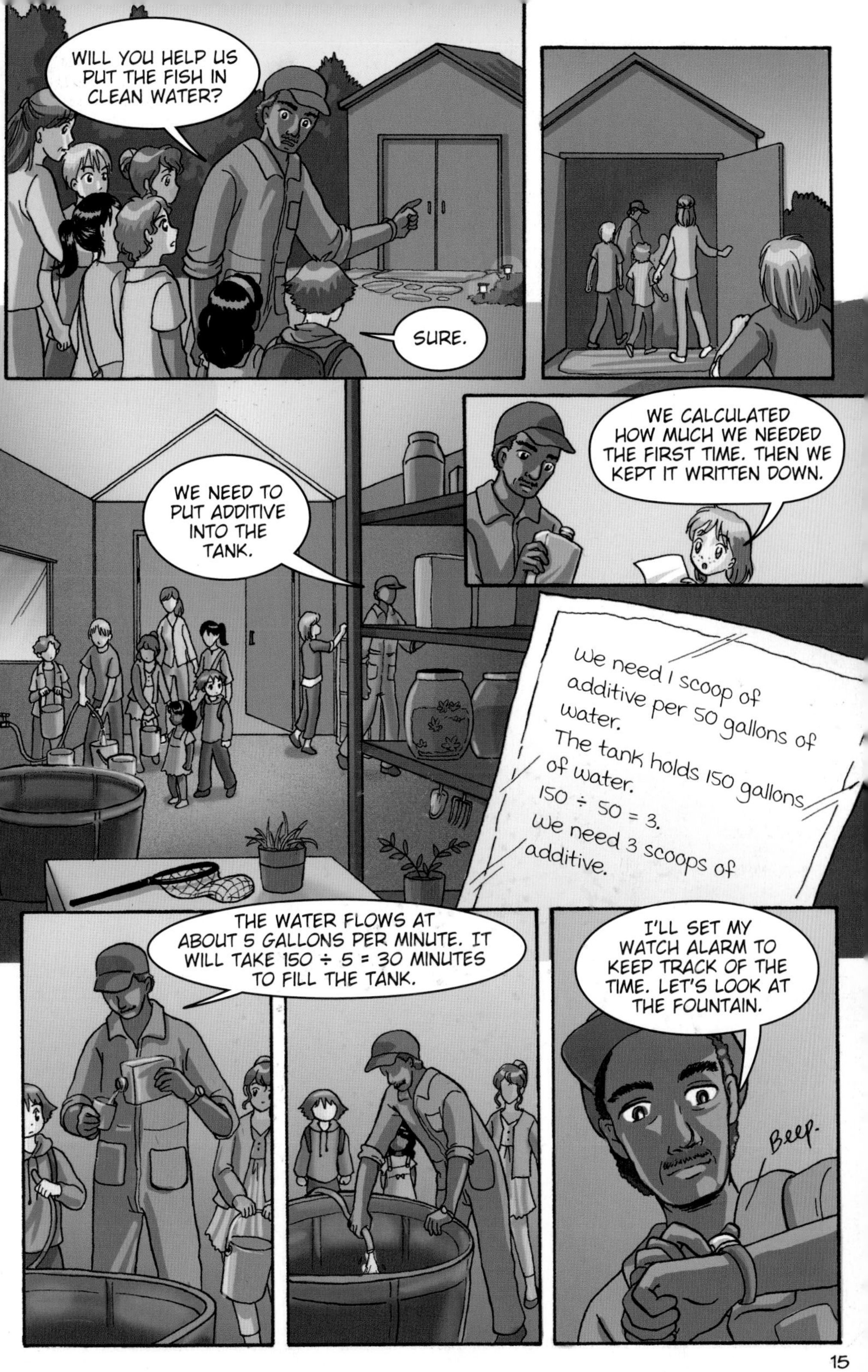
WILL YOU HELP US PUT THE FISH IN CLEAN WATER?
SURE.
WE NEED TO PUT ADDITIVE INTO THE TANK.
WE CALCULATED HOW MUCH WE NEEDED THE FIRST TIME. THEN WE KEPT IT WRITTEN DOWN.
We need 1 scoop of additive per 50 gallons of water.
The tank holds 150 gallons of water.
150 ÷ 50 = 3.
We need 3 scoops of additive.
THE WATER FLOWS AT ABOUT 5 GALLONS PER MINUTE. IT WILL TAKE 150 ÷ 5 = 30 MINUTES TO FILL THE TANK.
I'LL SET MY WATCH ALARM TO KEEP TRACK OF THE TIME. LET'S LOOK AT THE FOUNTAIN.
Beep.

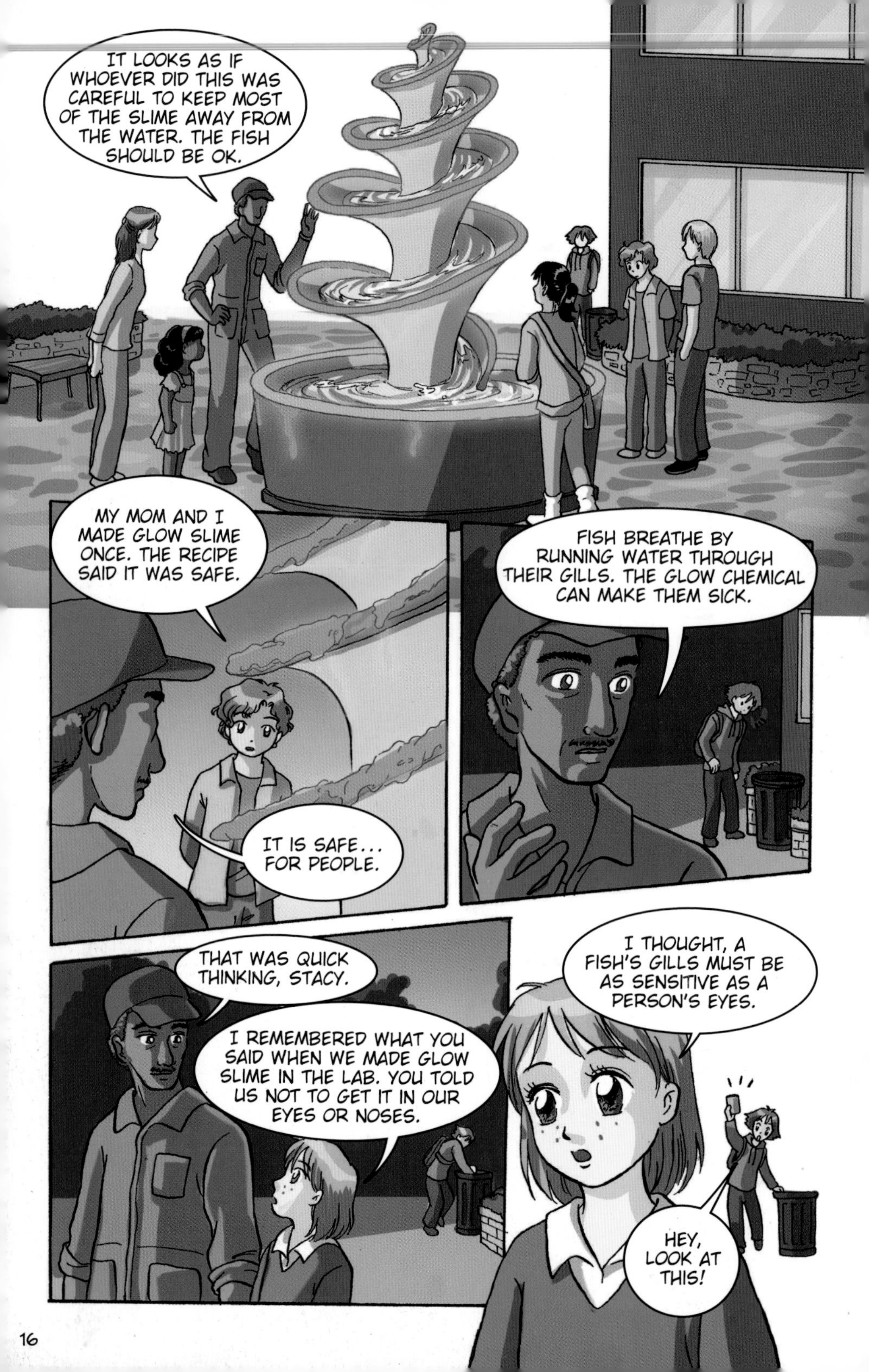
IT LOOKS AS IF WHOEVER DID THIS WAS CAREFUL TO KEEP MOST OF THE SLIME AWAY FROM THE WATER. THE FISH SHOULD BE OK.
MY MOM AND I MADE GLOW SLIME ONCE. THE RECIPE SAID IT WAS SAFE.
IT IS SAFE... FOR PEOPLE.
FISH BREATHE BY RUNNING WATER THROUGH THEIR GILLS. THE GLOW CHEMICAL CAN MAKE THEM SICK.
THAT WAS QUICK THINKING, STACY.
I REMEMBERED WHAT YOU SAID WHEN WE MADE GLOW SLIME IN THE LAB. YOU TOLD US NOT TO GET IT IN OUR EYES OR NOSES.
I THOUGHT, A FISH'S GILLS MUST BE AS SENSITIVE AS A PERSON'S EYES.
HEY, LOOK AT THIS!

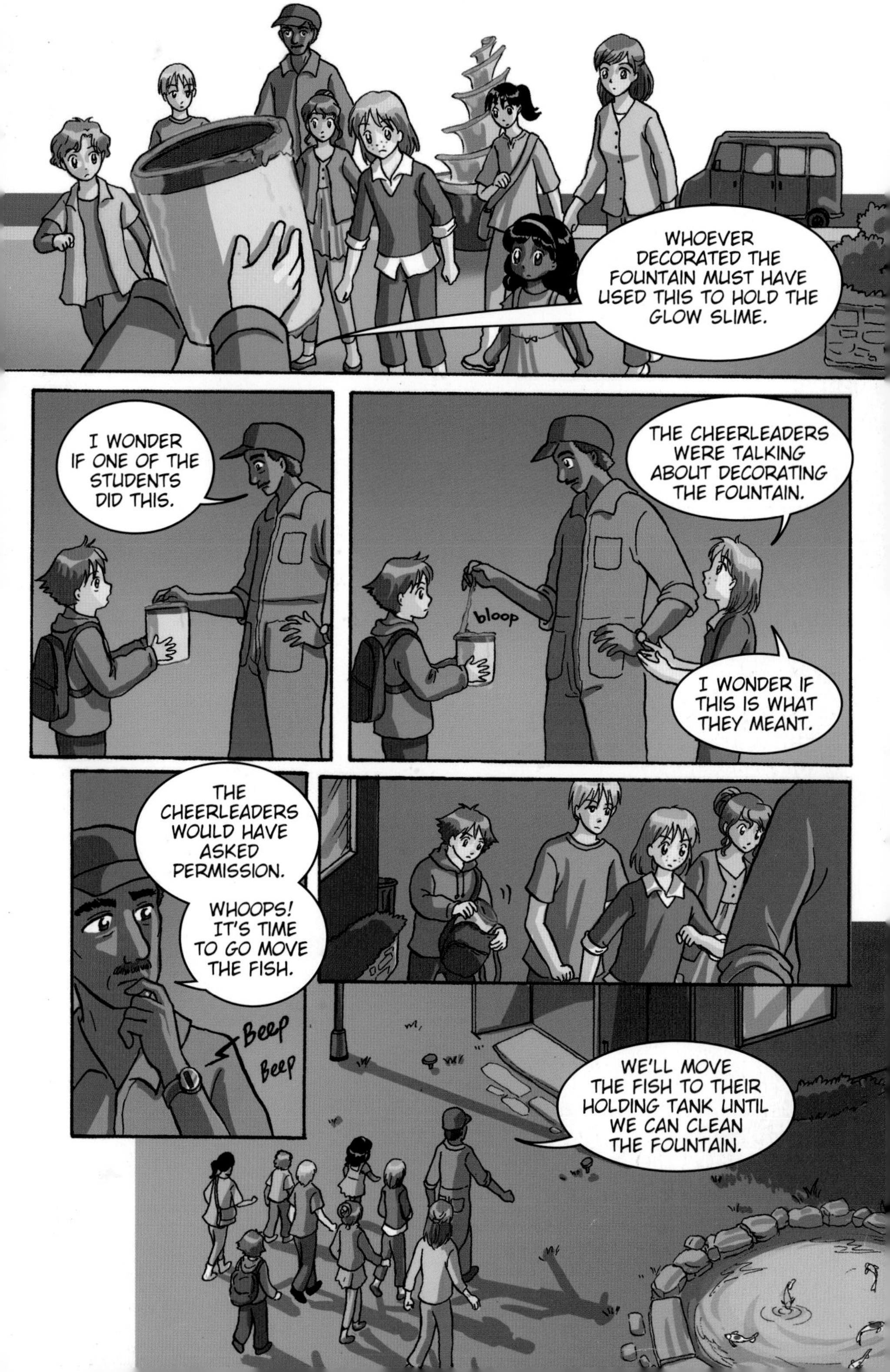
WHOEVER DECORATED THE FOUNTAIN MUST HAVE USED THIS TO HOLD THE GLOW SLIME.
I WONDER IF ONE OF THE STUDENTS DID THIS.
THE CHEERLEADERS WERE TALKING ABOUT DECORATING THE FOUNTAIN.
bloop
I WONDER IF THIS IS WHAT THEY MEANT.
THE CHEERLEADERS WOULD HAVE ASKED PERMISSION.
WHOOPS! IT'S TIME TO GO MOVE THE FISH.
Beep
Beep
WE'LL MOVE THE FISH TO THEIR HOLDING TANK UNTIL WE CAN CLEAN THE FOUNTAIN.

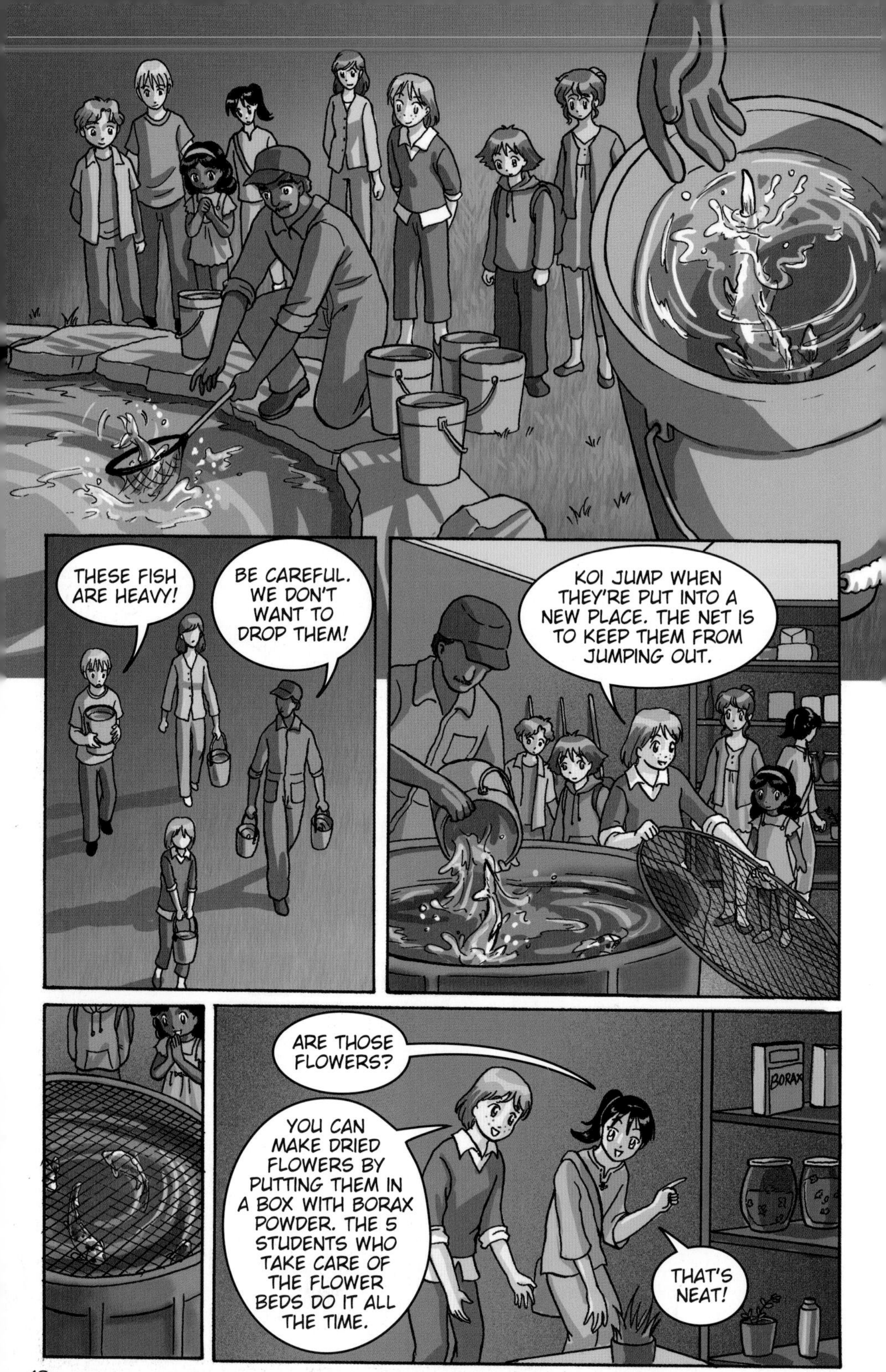
THESE FISH ARE HEAVY!
BE CAREFUL. WE DON'T WANT TO DROP THEM!
KOI JUMP WHEN THEY'RE PUT INTO A NEW PLACE. THE NET IS TO KEEP THEM FROM JUMPING OUT.
ARE THOSE FLOWERS?
YOU CAN MAKE DRIED FLOWERS BY PUTTING THEM IN A BOX WITH BORAX POWDER. THE 5 STUDENTS WHO TAKE CARE OF THE FLOWER BEDS DO IT ALL THE TIME.
THAT'S NEAT!
BORAX

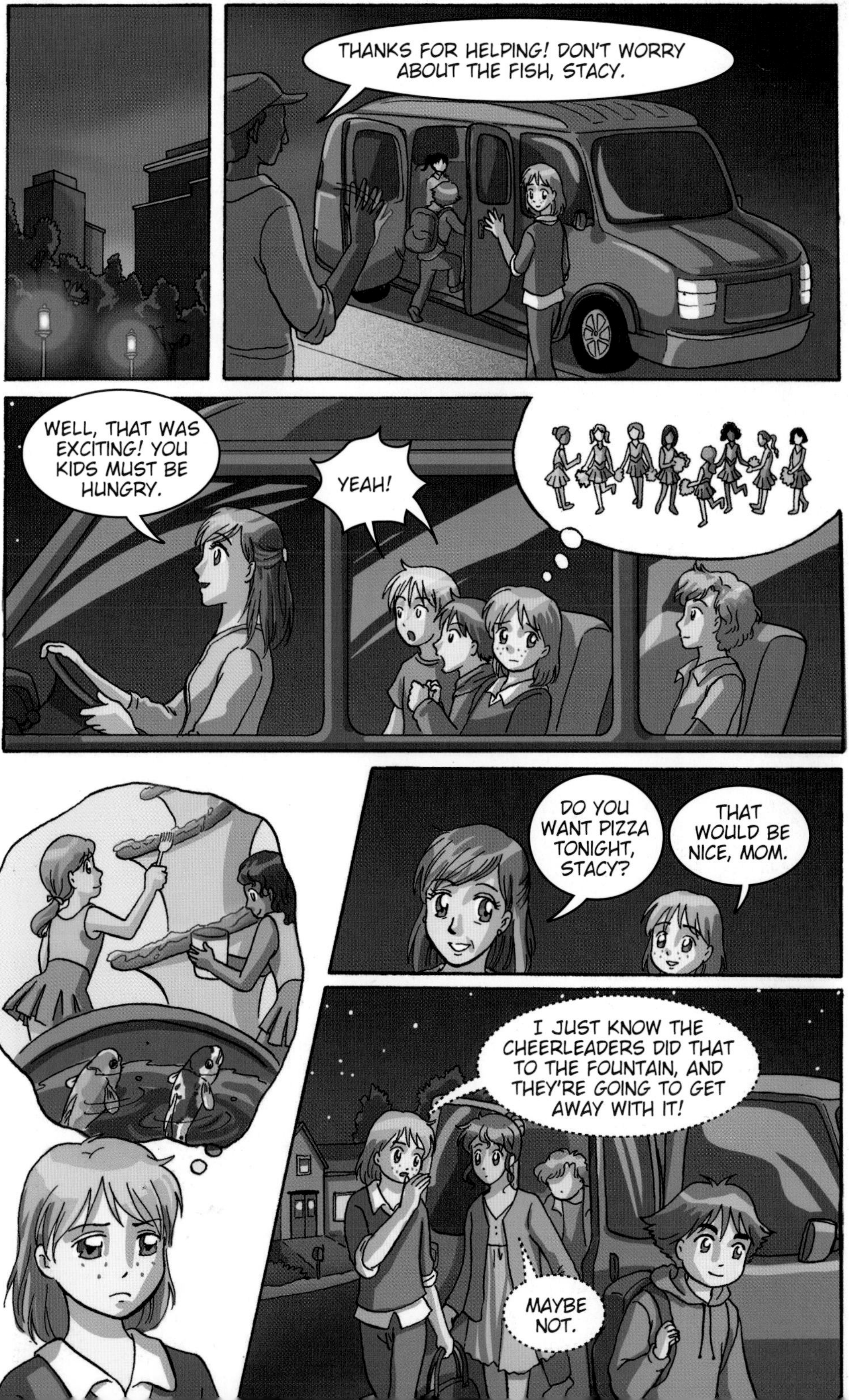
THANKS FOR HELPING! DON'T WORRY ABOUT THE FISH, STACY.
WELL, THAT WAS EXCITING! YOU KIDS MUST BE HUNGRY.
YEAH!
DO YOU WANT PIZZA TONIGHT, STACY?
THAT WOULD BE NICE, MOM.
I JUST KNOW THE CHEERLEADERS DID THAT TO THE FOUNTAIN, AND THEY'RE GOING TO GET AWAY WITH IT!
MAYBE NOT.

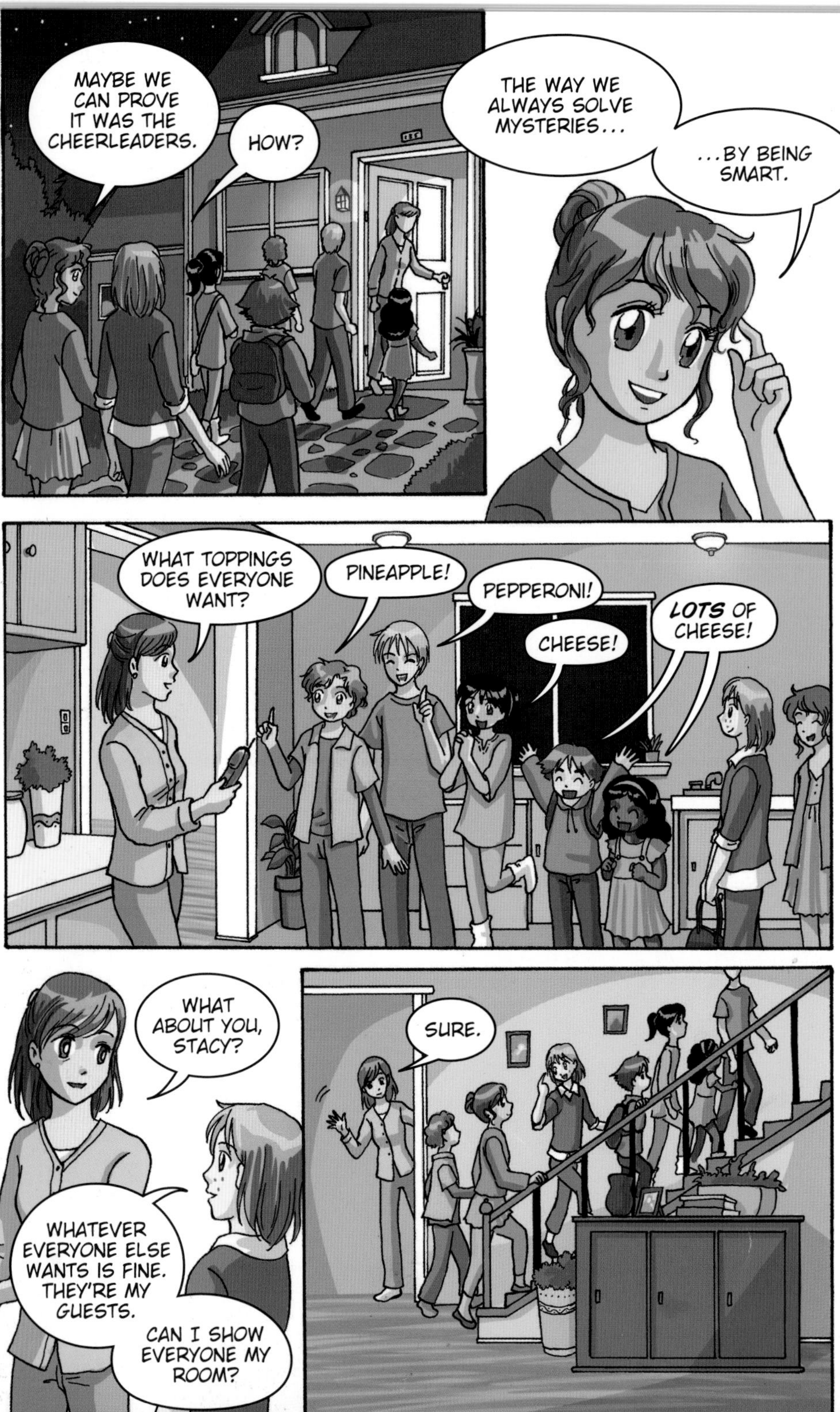
MAYBE WE CAN PROVE IT WAS THE CHEERLEADERS.
HOW?
THE WAY WE ALWAYS SOLVE MYSTERIES...
...BY BEING SMART.
WHAT TOPPINGS DOES EVERYONE WANT?
PINEAPPLE!
PEPPERONI!
CHEESE!
LOTS OF CHEESE!
WHAT ABOUT YOU, STACY?
WHATEVER EVERYONE ELSE WANTS IS FINE. THEY'RE MY GUESTS.
CAN I SHOW EVERYONE MY ROOM?
SURE.

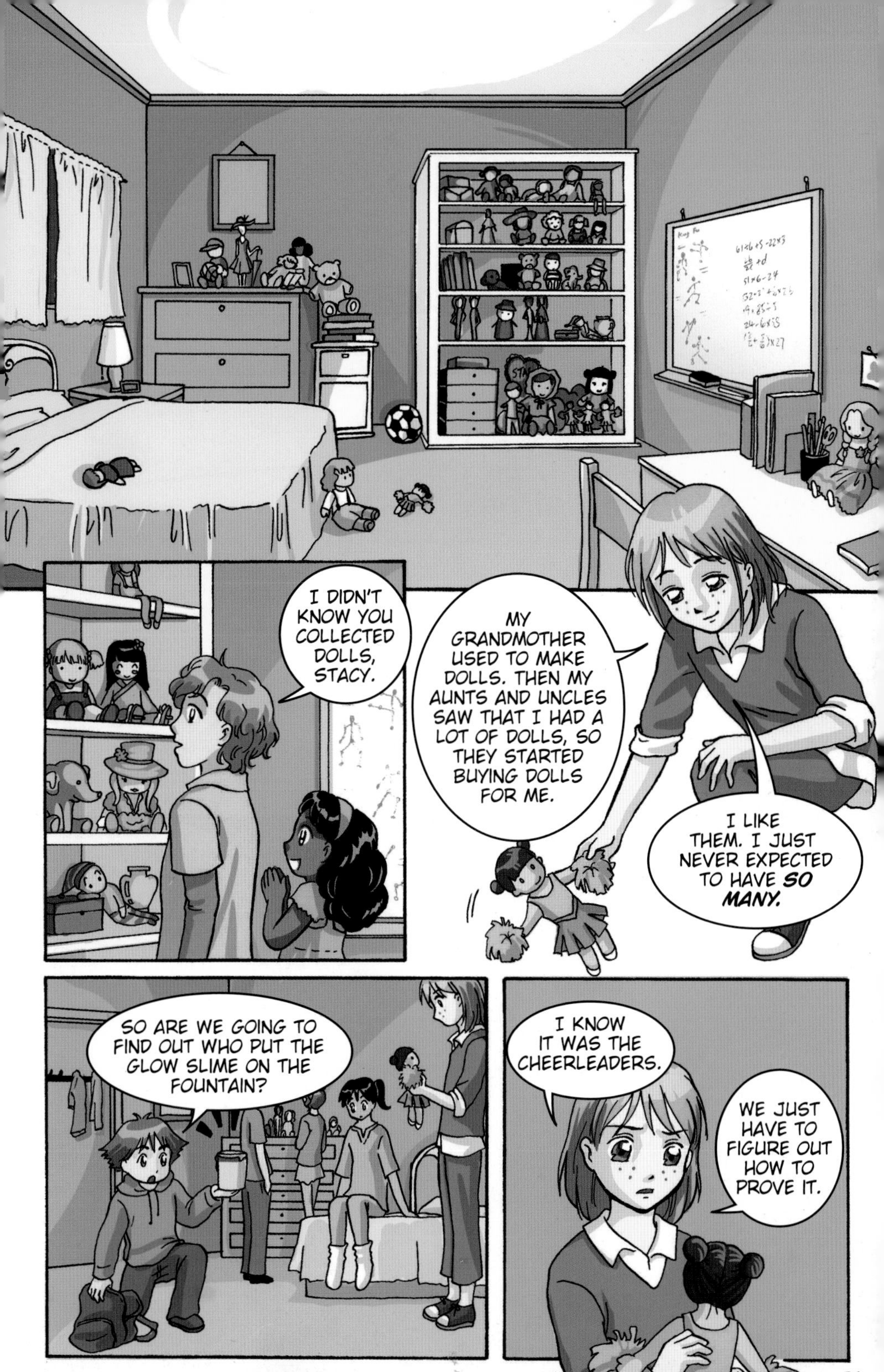
I DIDN'T KNOW YOU COLLECTED DOLLS, STACY.
MY GRANDMOTHER USED TO MAKE DOLLS. THEN MY AUNTS AND UNCLES SAW THAT I HAD A LOT OF DOLLS, SO THEY STARTED BUYING DOLLS FOR ME.
I LIKE THEM. I JUST NEVER EXPECTED TO HAVE ***SO MANY.***
SO ARE WE GOING TO FIND OUT WHO PUT THE GLOW SLIME ON THE FOUNTAIN?
I KNOW IT WAS THE CHEERLEADERS.
WE JUST HAVE TO FIGURE OUT HOW TO PROVE IT.

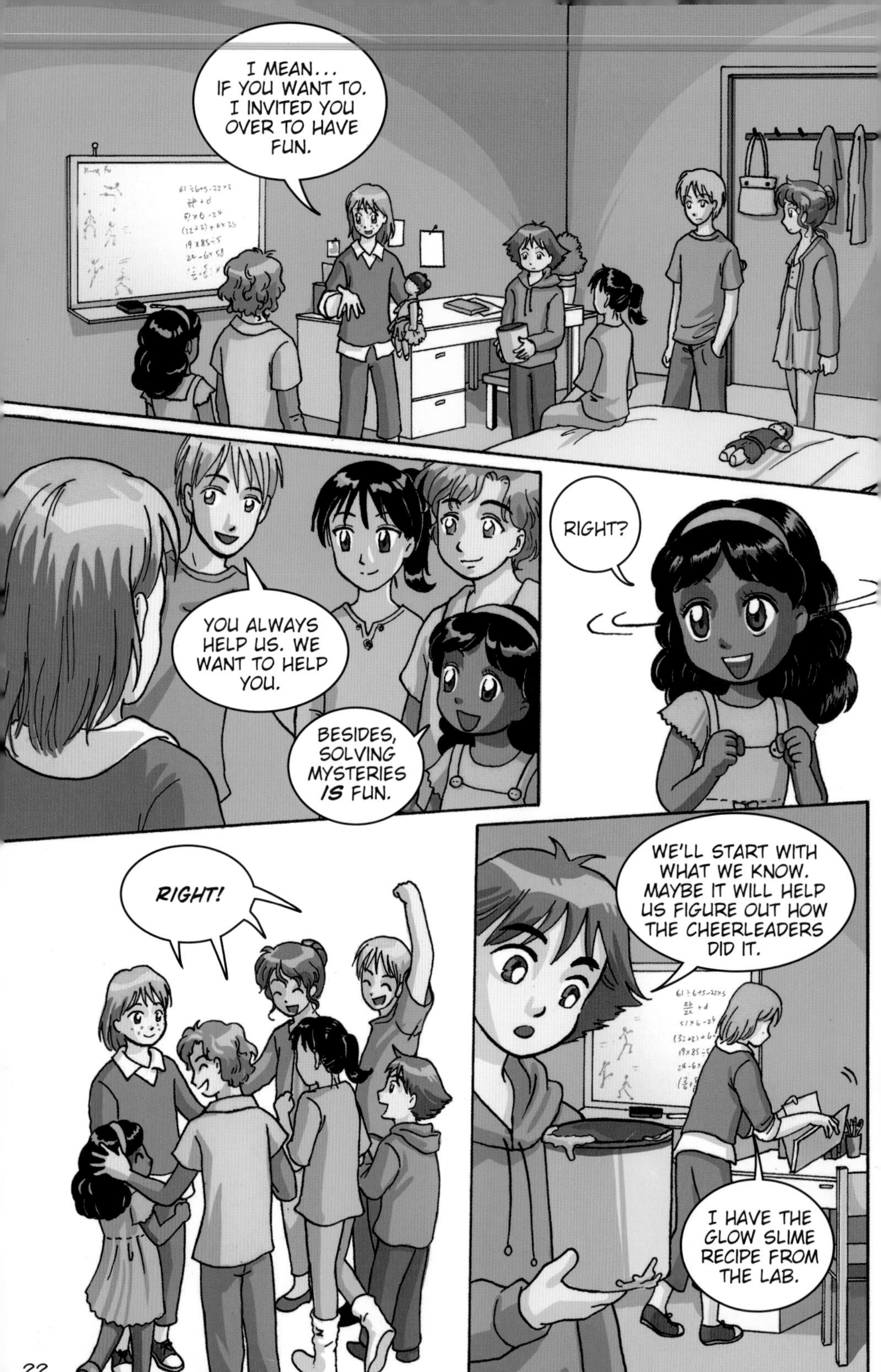
I MEAN... IF YOU WANT TO. I INVITED YOU OVER TO HAVE FUN.
YOU ALWAYS HELP US. WE WANT TO HELP YOU.
BESIDES, SOLVING MYSTERIES *IS* FUN.
RIGHT?
RIGHT!
WE'LL START WITH WHAT WE KNOW. MAYBE IT WILL HELP US FIGURE OUT HOW THE CHEERLEADERS DID IT.
I HAVE THE GLOW SLIME RECIPE FROM THE LAB.

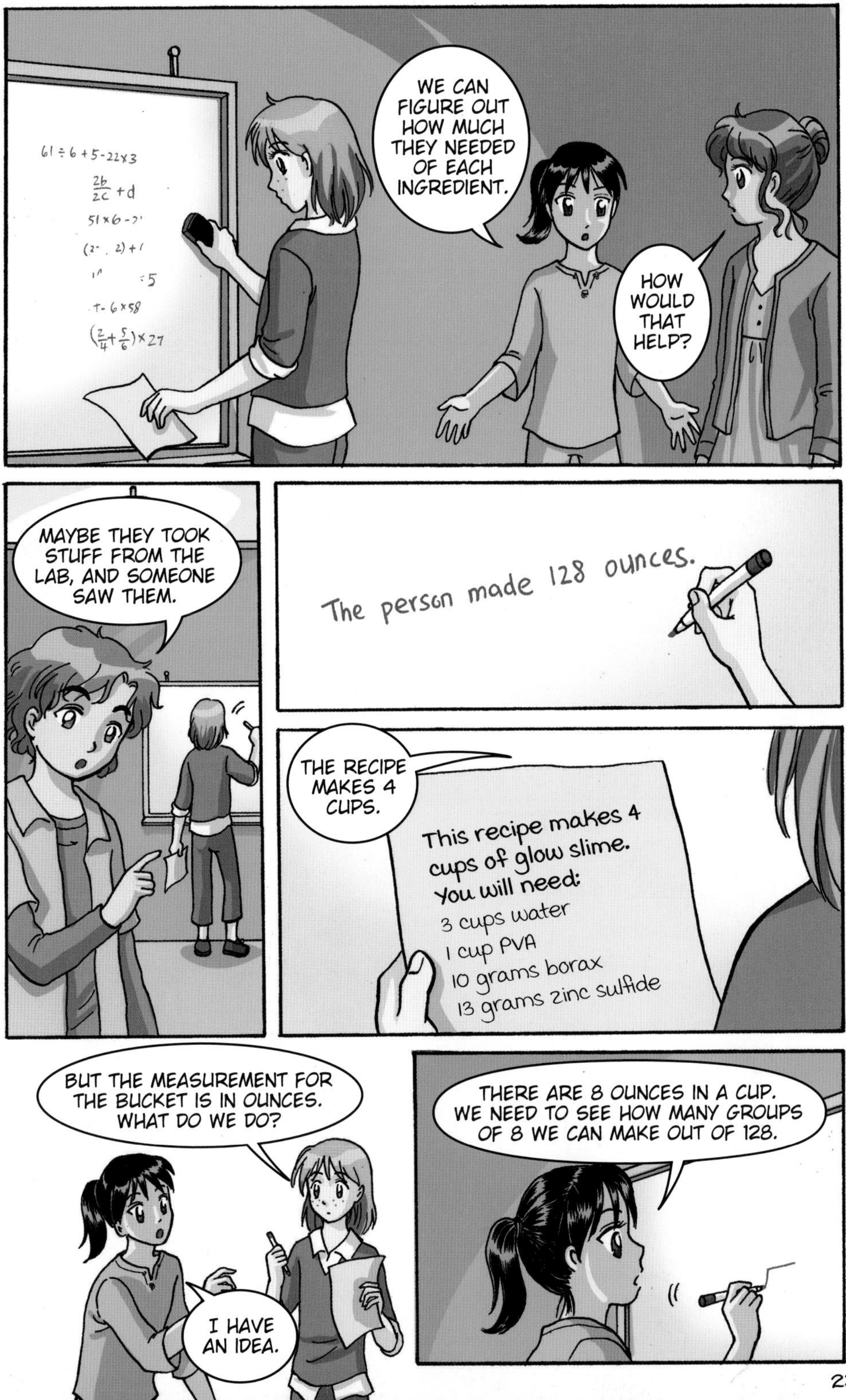
WE CAN FIGURE OUT HOW MUCH THEY NEEDED OF EACH INGREDIENT.
HOW WOULD THAT HELP?
MAYBE THEY TOOK STUFF FROM THE LAB, AND SOMEONE SAW THEM.
The person made 128 ounces.
THE RECIPE MAKES 4 CUPS.
This recipe makes 4 cups of glow slime.
You will need:
3 cups water
1 cup PVA
10 grams borax
13 grams zinc sulfide
BUT THE MEASUREMENT FOR THE BUCKET IS IN OUNCES. WHAT DO WE DO?
I HAVE AN IDEA.
THERE ARE 8 OUNCES IN A CUP. WE NEED TO SEE HOW MANY GROUPS OF 8 WE CAN MAKE OUT OF 128.

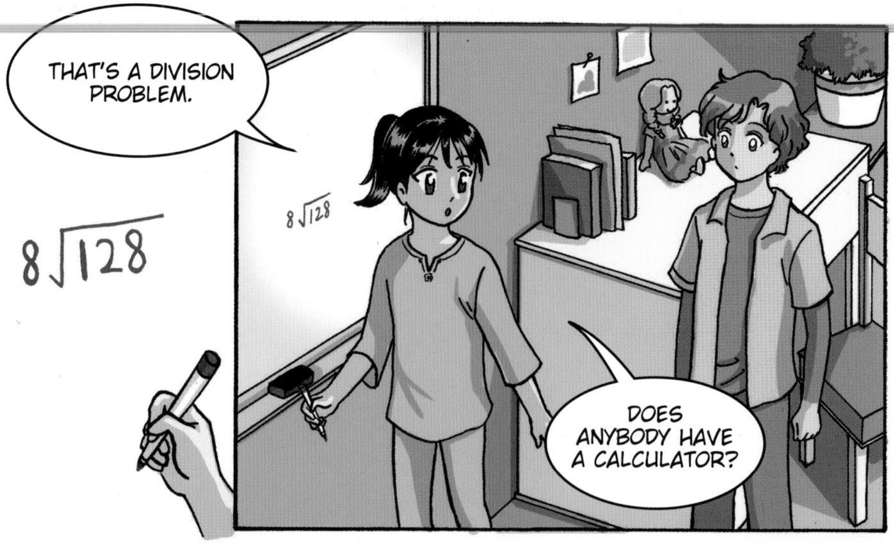
THAT'S A DIVISION PROBLEM.
8 √128
DOES ANYBODY HAVE A CALCULATOR?

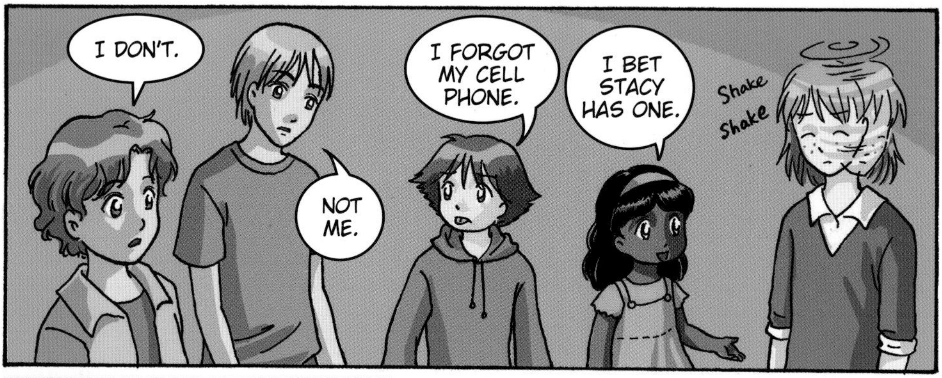
I DON'T.
NOT ME.
I FORGOT MY CELL PHONE.
I BET STACY HAS ONE.
Shake
Shake

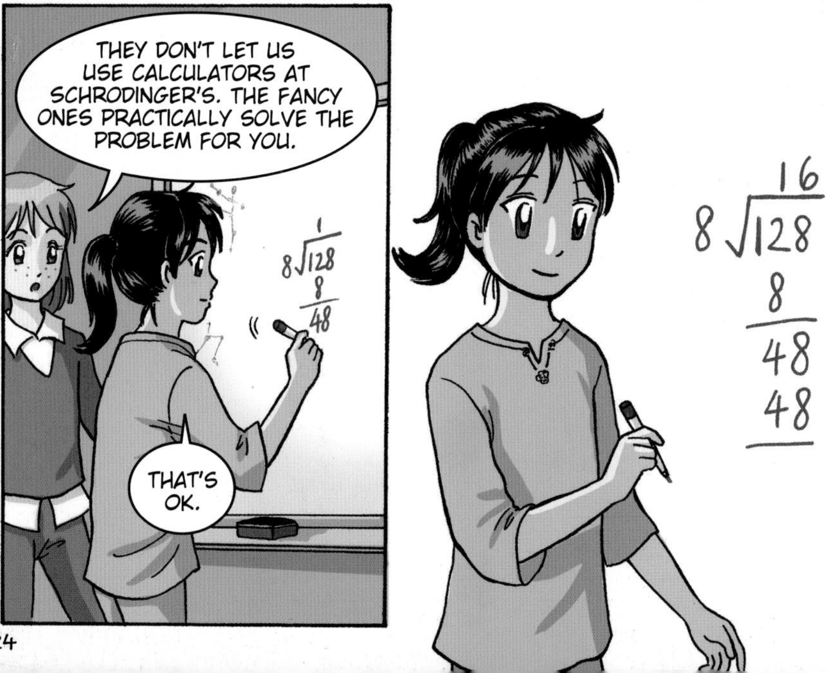
THEY DON'T LET US USE CALCULATORS AT SCHRODINGER'S. THE FANCY ONES PRACTICALLY SOLVE THE PROBLEM FOR YOU.
THAT'S OK.
16
8 √128
8
48
48

OK, NOW WE KNOW THAT THE PERSON USED 16 CUPS OF GLOW SLIME, BUT THE RECIPE MAKES 4 CUPS. NOW WHAT?

NOW WE FIGURE OUT HOW MANY TIMES THEY WOULD HAVE HAD TO MAKE THE RECIPE TO GET 16 CUPS.

This recipe makes 4 cups of glow slime.

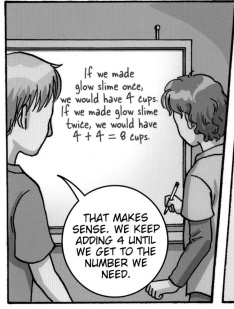

If we made glow slime once, we would have 4 cups. If we made glow slime twice, we would have 4 + 4 = 8 cups.

THAT MAKES SENSE. WE KEEP ADDING 4 UNTIL WE GET TO THE NUMBER WE NEED.

If we made glow slime once, we would have 4 cups. If we made glow slime twice, we would have 4 + 4 = 8 cups.

3 times would make 4 + 4 + 4 = 12 cups.

4 times would make 4 + 4 + 4 + 4 = 16 cups.

THEY HAD TO MAKE THE RECIPE 4 TIMES TO GET 16 CUPS OF SLIME.

THAT MEANS THEY NEEDED 4 TIMES AS MUCH STUFF.

25

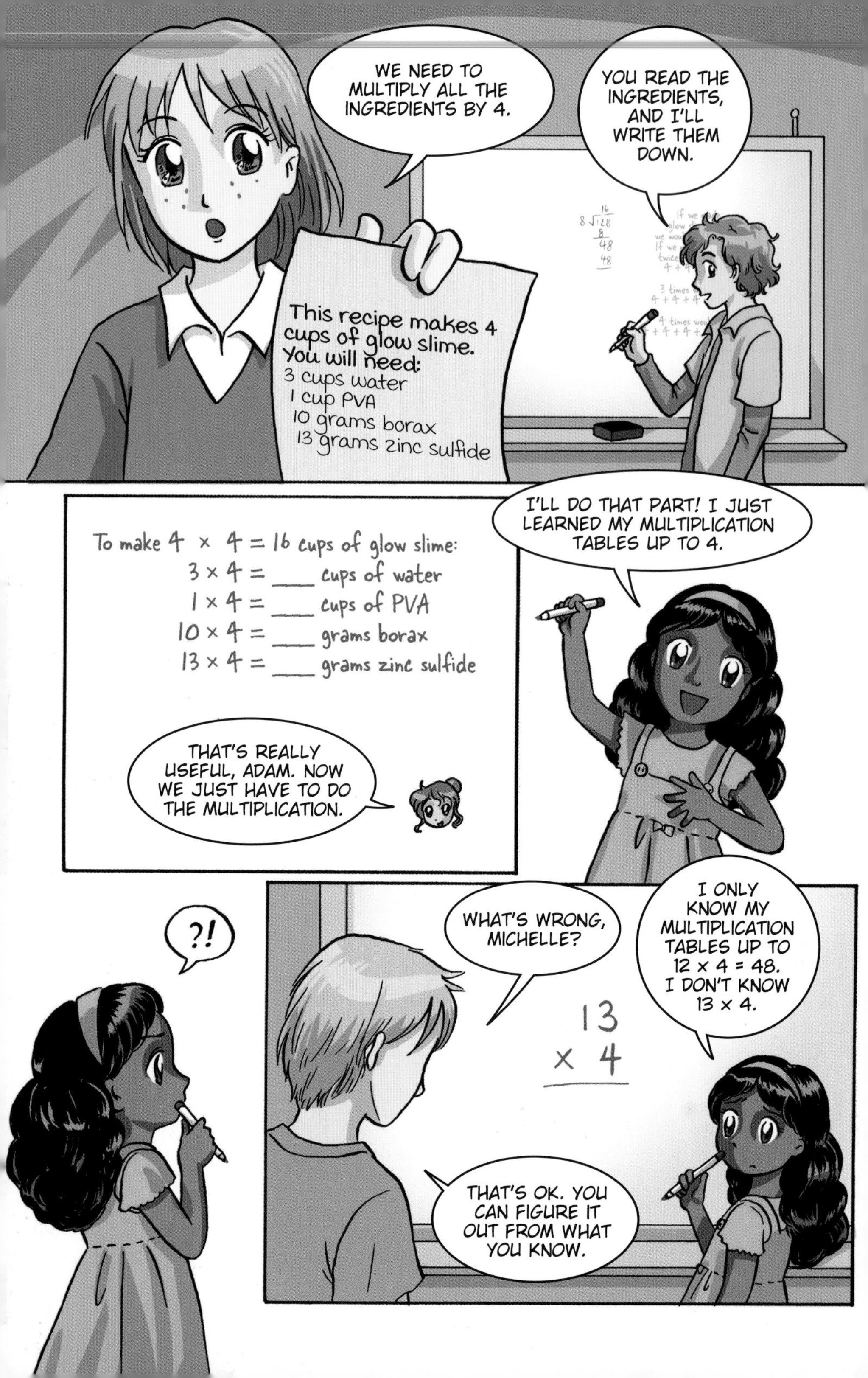
WE NEED TO MULTIPLY ALL THE INGREDIENTS BY 4.
YOU READ THE INGREDIENTS, AND I'LL WRITE THEM DOWN.
This recipe makes 4 cups of glow slime. You will need:
3 cups water
1 cup PVA
10 grams borax
13 grams zinc sulfide
To make 4 × 4 = 16 cups of glow slime:
3 × 4 = ___ cups of water
1 × 4 = ___ cups of PVA
10 × 4 = ___ grams borax
13 × 4 = ___ grams zinc sulfide
THAT'S REALLY USEFUL, ADAM. NOW WE JUST HAVE TO DO THE MULTIPLICATION.
I'LL DO THAT PART! I JUST LEARNED MY MULTIPLICATION TABLES UP TO 4.
?!
WHAT'S WRONG, MICHELLE?
I ONLY KNOW MY MULTIPLICATION TABLES UP TO 12 × 4 = 48. I DON'T KNOW 13 × 4.
13 × 4
THAT'S OK. YOU CAN FIGURE IT OUT FROM WHAT YOU KNOW.

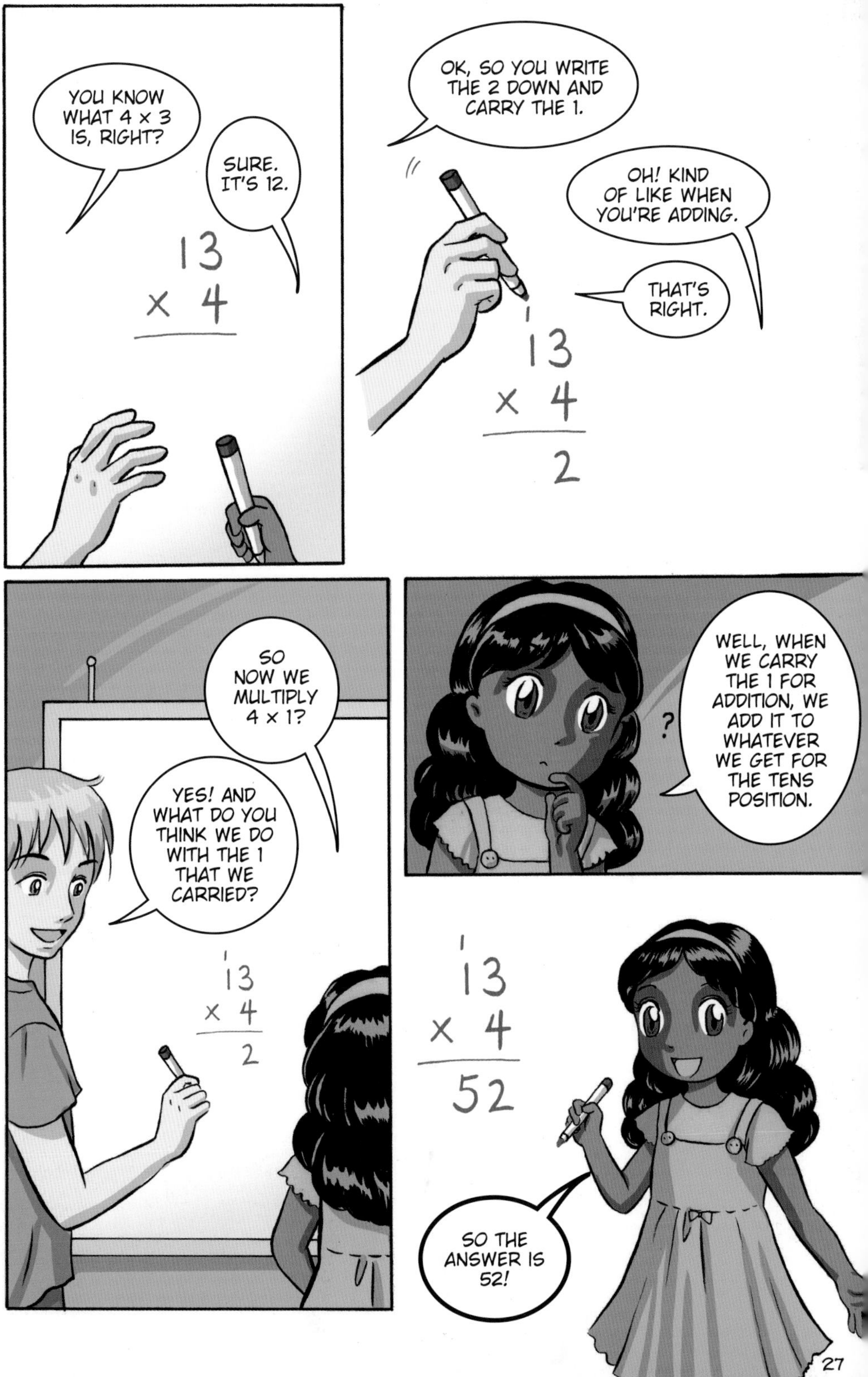
YOU KNOW WHAT 4 x 3 IS, RIGHT?
SURE. IT'S 12.
13
x 4
OK, SO YOU WRITE THE 2 DOWN AND CARRY THE 1.
OH! KIND OF LIKE WHEN YOU'RE ADDING.
THAT'S RIGHT.
1
13
x 4
2
SO NOW WE MULTIPLY 4 x 1?
YES! AND WHAT DO YOU THINK WE DO WITH THE 1 THAT WE CARRIED?
1
13
x 4
2
?
WELL, WHEN WE CARRY THE 1 FOR ADDITION, WE ADD IT TO WHATEVER WE GET FOR THE TENS POSITION.
1
13
x 4
52
SO THE ANSWER IS 52!

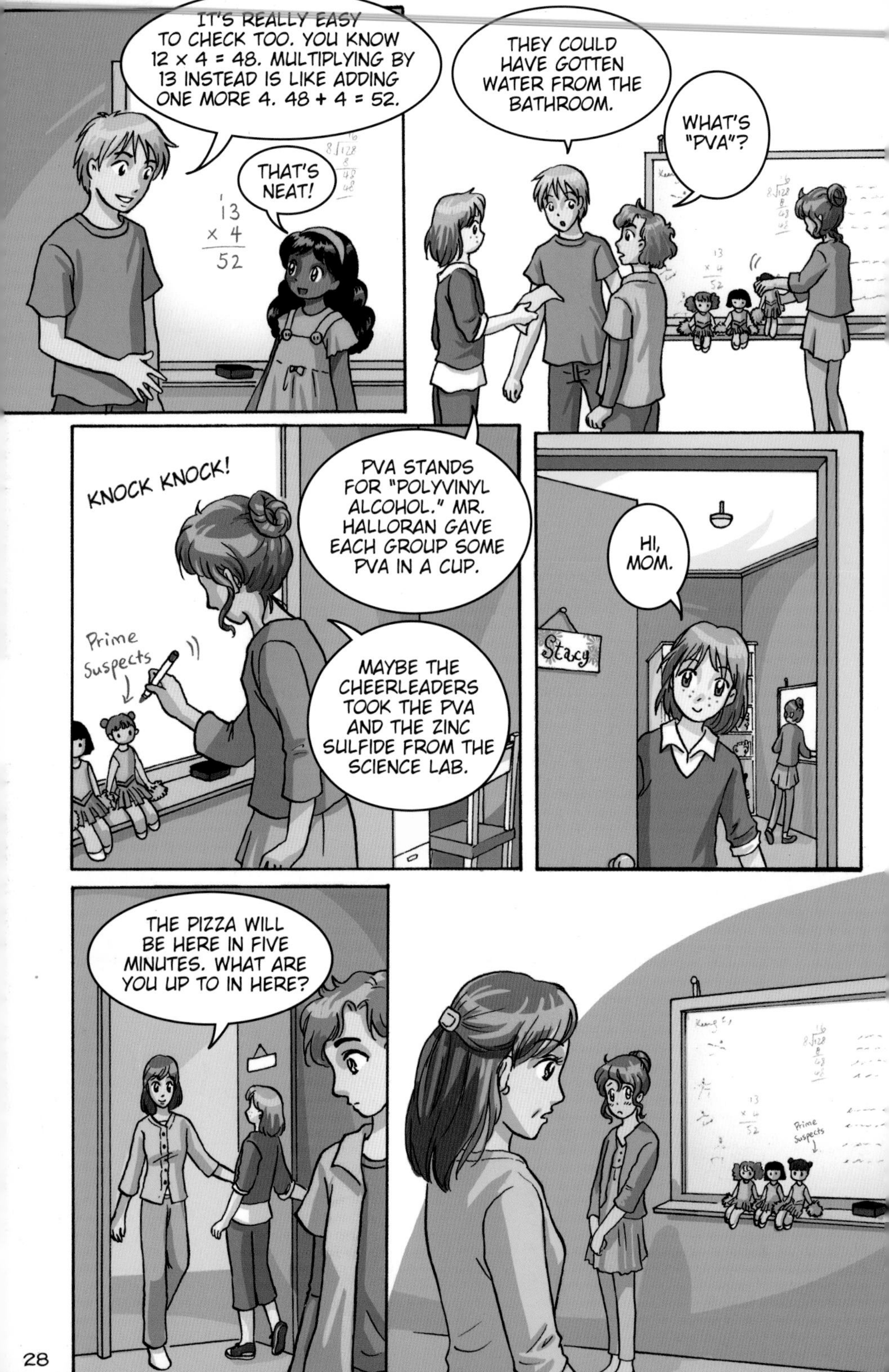
IT'S REALLY EASY TO CHECK TOO. YOU KNOW 12 x 4 = 48. MULTIPLYING BY 13 INSTEAD IS LIKE ADDING ONE MORE 4. 48 + 4 = 52.
THAT'S NEAT!
13 x 4 = 52
THEY COULD HAVE GOTTEN WATER FROM THE BATHROOM.
WHAT'S "PVA"?
KNOCK KNOCK!
PVA STANDS FOR "POLYVINYL ALCOHOL." MR. HALLORAN GAVE EACH GROUP SOME PVA IN A CUP.
MAYBE THE CHEERLEADERS TOOK THE PVA AND THE ZINC SULFIDE FROM THE SCIENCE LAB.
Prime Suspects
HI, MOM.
Stacy
THE PIZZA WILL BE HERE IN FIVE MINUTES. WHAT ARE YOU UP TO IN HERE?
Prime Suspects

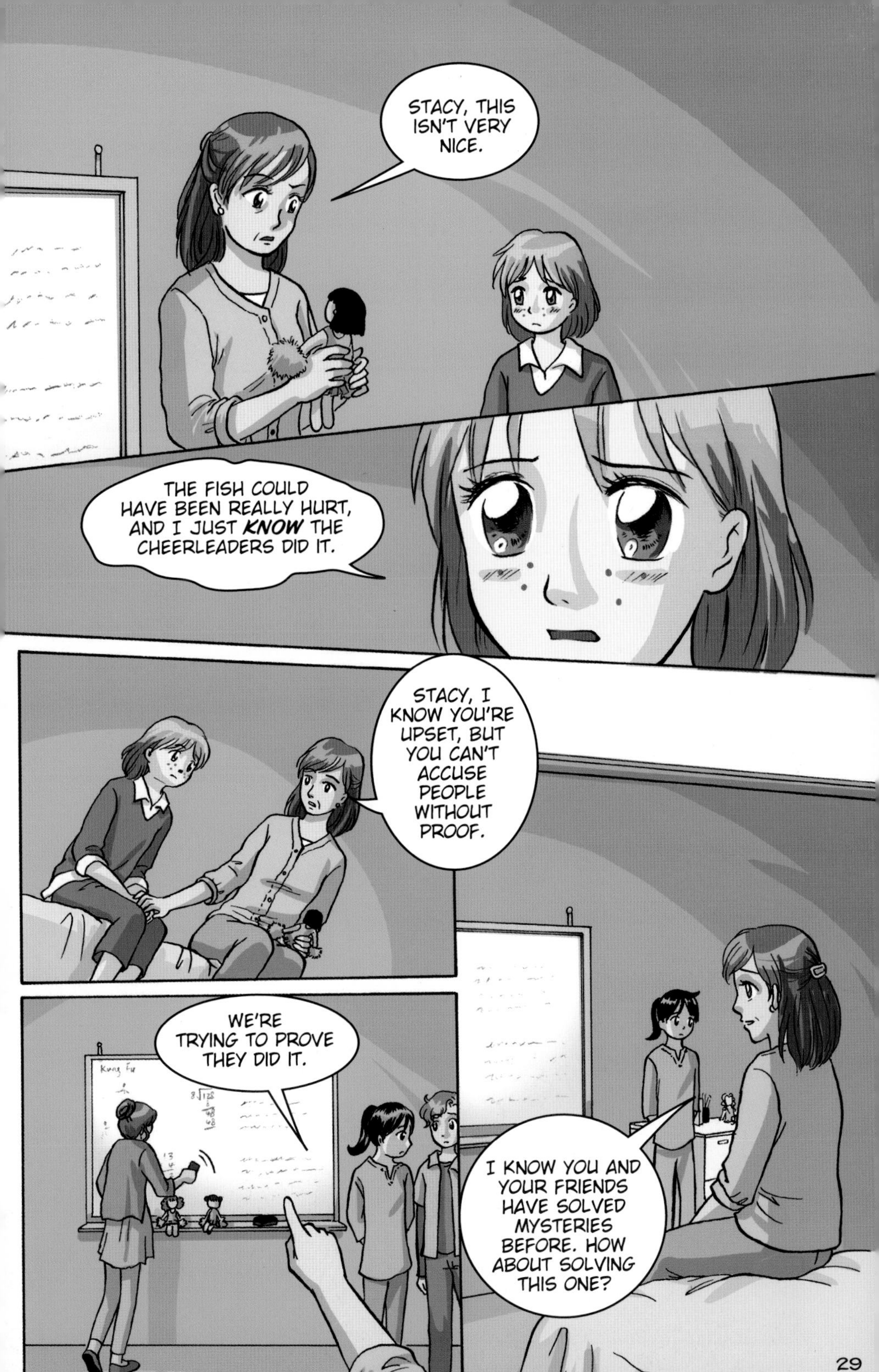
STACY, THIS ISN'T VERY NICE.
THE FISH COULD HAVE BEEN REALLY HURT, AND I JUST ***KNOW*** THE CHEERLEADERS DID IT.
STACY, I KNOW YOU'RE UPSET, BUT YOU CAN'T ACCUSE PEOPLE WITHOUT PROOF.
WE'RE TRYING TO PROVE THEY DID IT.
I KNOW YOU AND YOUR FRIENDS HAVE SOLVED MYSTERIES BEFORE. HOW ABOUT SOLVING THIS ONE?

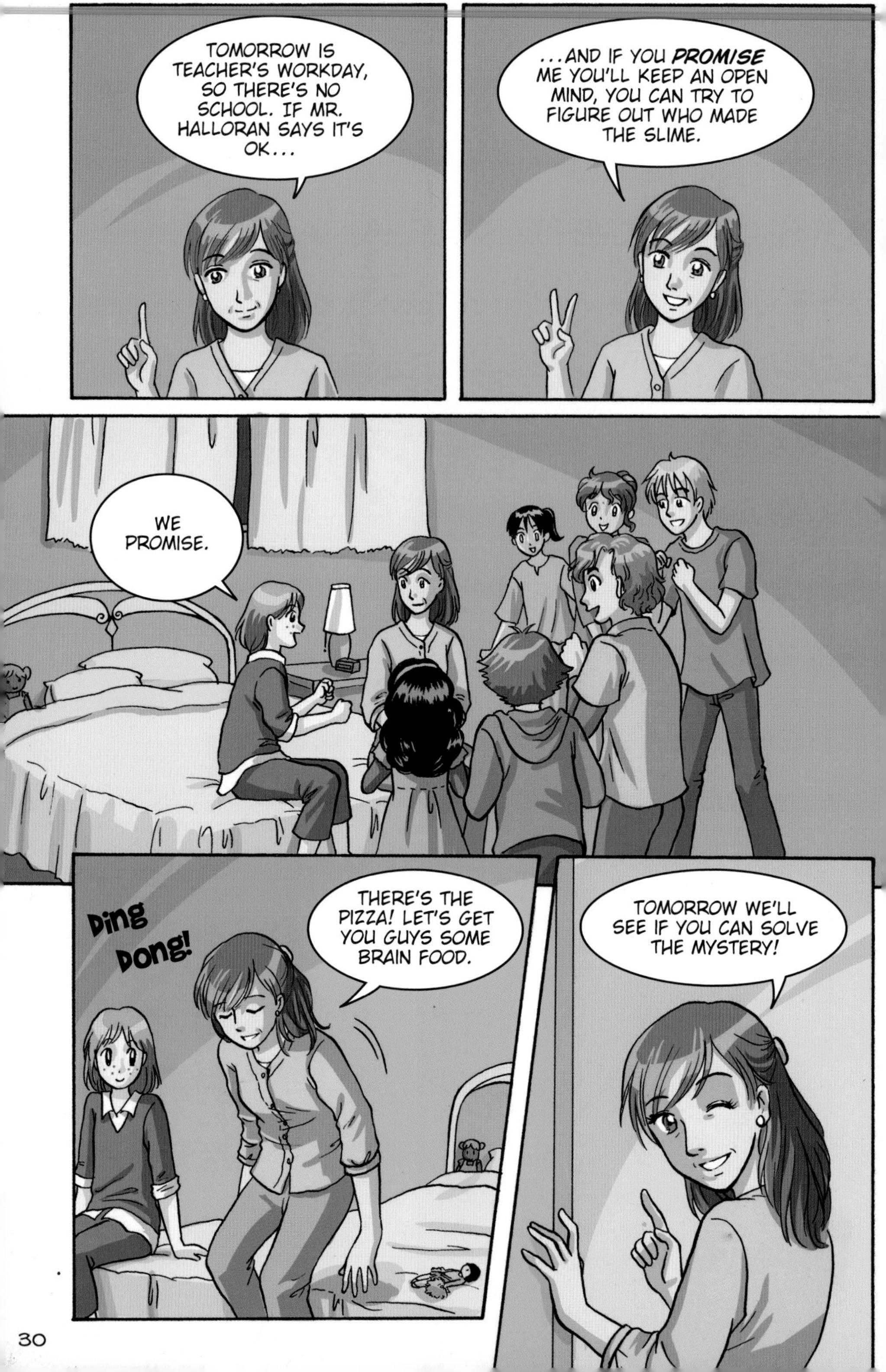
TOMORROW IS TEACHER'S WORKDAY, SO THERE'S NO SCHOOL. IF MR. HALLORAN SAYS IT'S OK...
...AND IF YOU ***PROMISE*** ME YOU'LL KEEP AN OPEN MIND, YOU CAN TRY TO FIGURE OUT WHO MADE THE SLIME.
WE PROMISE.
Ding Dong!
THERE'S THE PIZZA! LET'S GET YOU GUYS SOME BRAIN FOOD.
TOMORROW WE'LL SEE IF YOU CAN SOLVE THE MYSTERY!

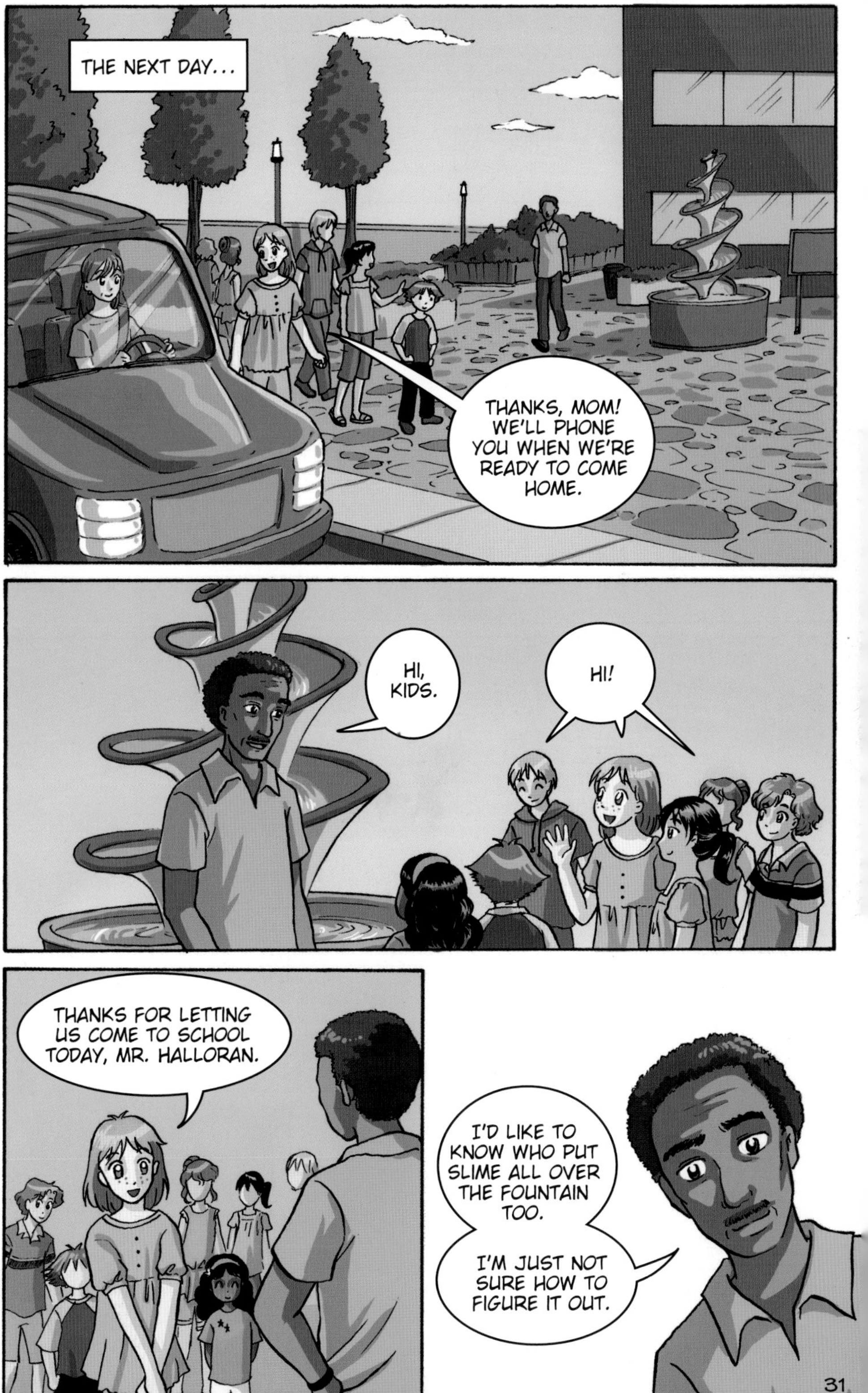
THE NEXT DAY...
THANKS, MOM! WE'LL PHONE YOU WHEN WE'RE READY TO COME HOME.
HI, KIDS.
HI!
THANKS FOR LETTING US COME TO SCHOOL TODAY, MR. HALLORAN.
I'D LIKE TO KNOW WHO PUT SLIME ALL OVER THE FOUNTAIN TOO.
I'M JUST NOT SURE HOW TO FIGURE IT OUT.

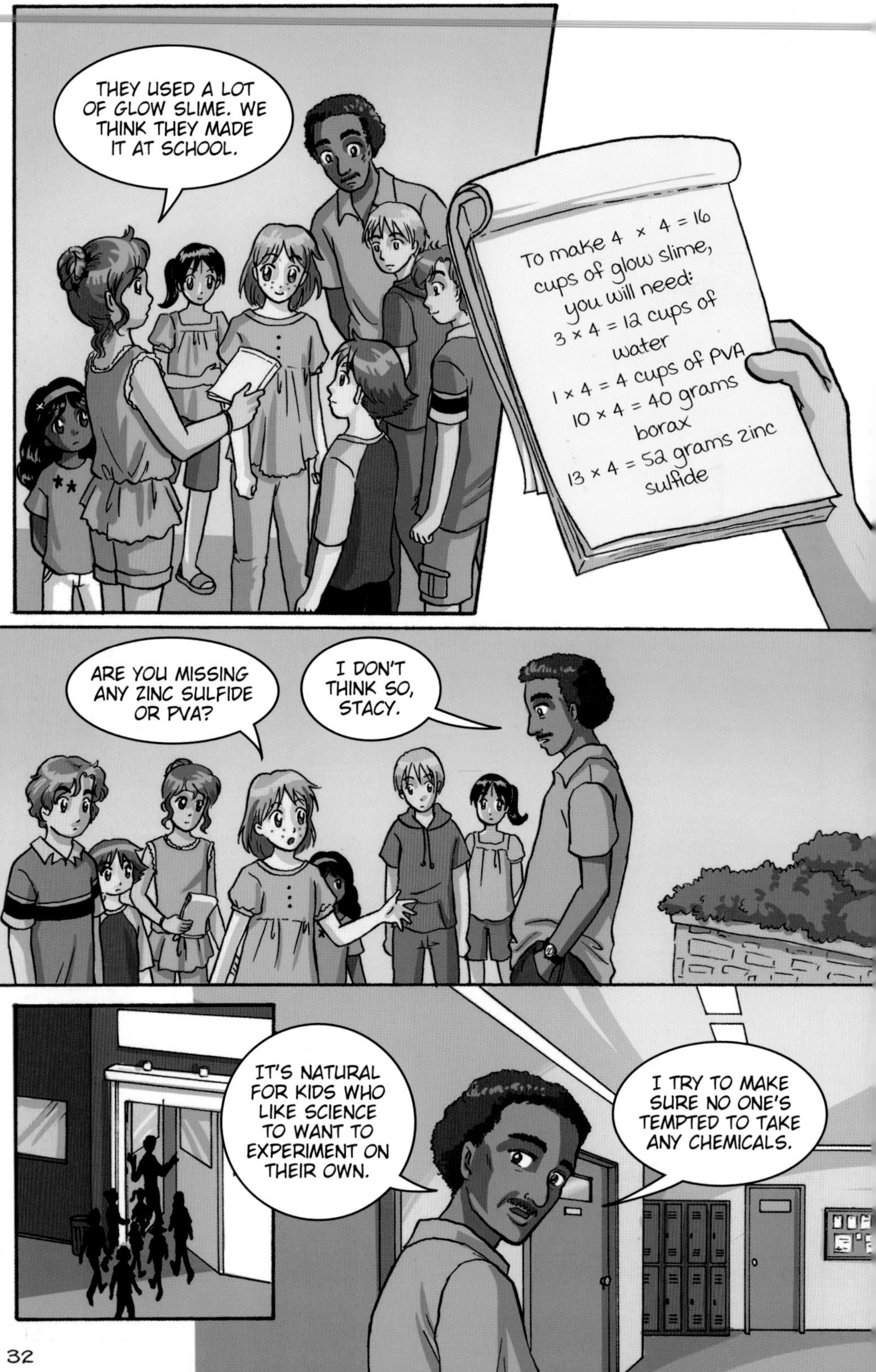
THEY USED A LOT OF GLOW SLIME. WE THINK THEY MADE IT AT SCHOOL.
To make 4 × 4 = 16 cups of glow slime, you will need:
3 × 4 = 12 cups of water
1 × 4 = 4 cups of PVA
10 × 4 = 40 grams borax
13 × 4 = 52 grams zinc sulfide
ARE YOU MISSING ANY ZINC SULFIDE OR PVA?
I DON'T THINK SO, STACY.
IT'S NATURAL FOR KIDS WHO LIKE SCIENCE TO WANT TO EXPERIMENT ON THEIR OWN.
I TRY TO MAKE SURE NO ONE'S TEMPTED TO TAKE ANY CHEMICALS.

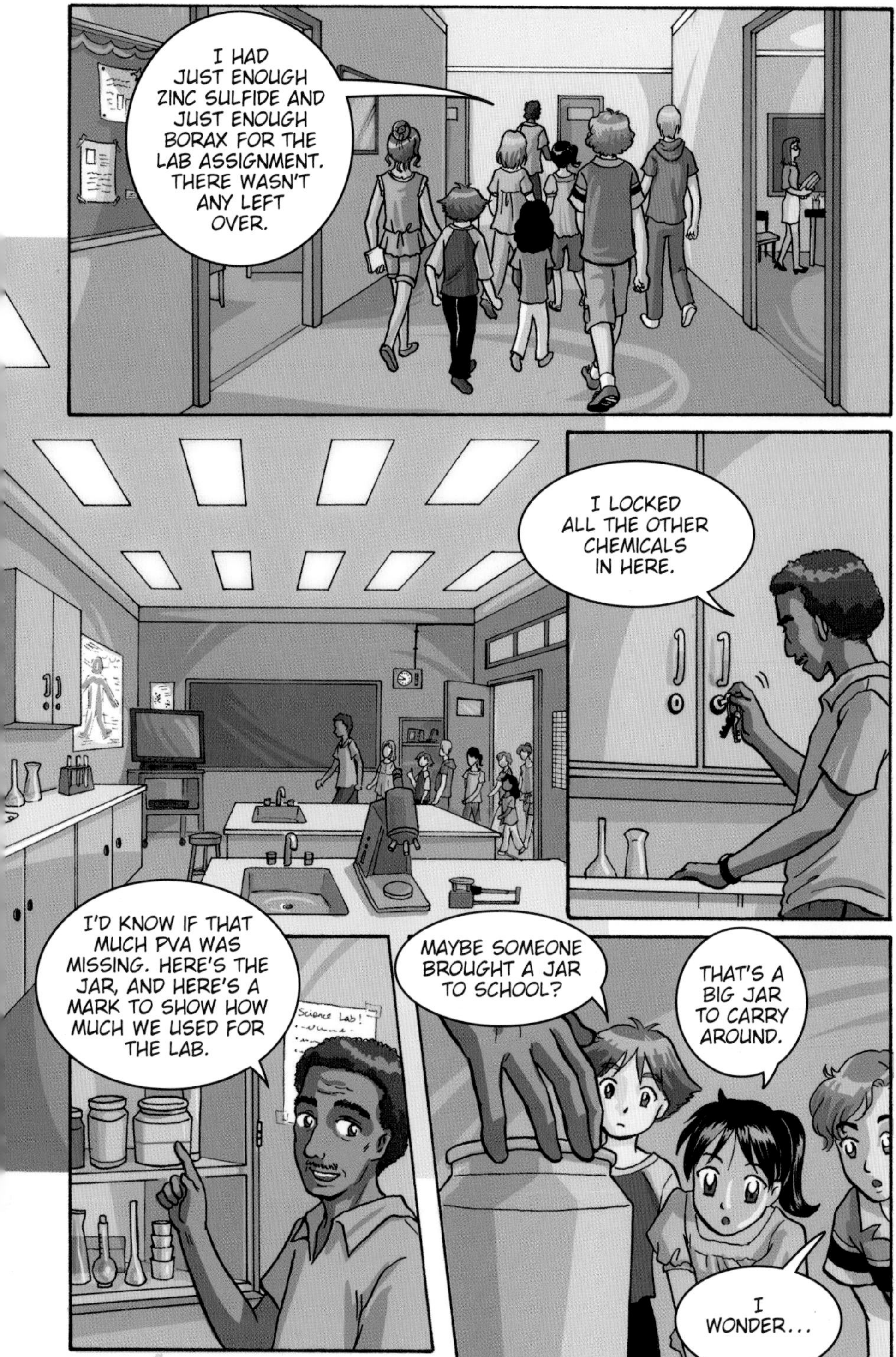

I HAD JUST ENOUGH ZINC SULFIDE AND JUST ENOUGH BORAX FOR THE LAB ASSIGNMENT. THERE WASN'T ANY LEFT OVER.
I LOCKED ALL THE OTHER CHEMICALS IN HERE.
I'D KNOW IF THAT MUCH PVA WAS MISSING. HERE'S THE JAR, AND HERE'S A MARK TO SHOW HOW MUCH WE USED FOR THE LAB.
Science Lab!
MAYBE SOMEONE BROUGHT A JAR TO SCHOOL?
THAT'S A BIG JAR TO CARRY AROUND.
I WONDER...

WHEN MY MOM AND I MADE GLOW SLIME, WE DIDN'T HAVE ANY PVA. THE RECIPE SAID WE COULD USE GLUE GEL INSTEAD.

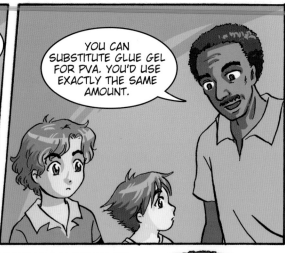

YOU CAN SUBSTITUTE GLUE GEL FOR PVA. YOU'D USE EXACTLY THE SAME AMOUNT.

I'LL WRITE DOWN THAT WE COULD USE PVA **OR** GLUE GEL.

WE HAVE GLUE GEL IN THE ART ROOM.

YOU HAVE AN ART ROOM? I THOUGHT YOUR SCHOOL WAS FOR SCIENCE AND MATH.

SCIENTISTS AND MATHEMATICIANS HAVE TO BE CREATIVE. JUST LIKE ARTISTS.

LOOK AT ALL THE CREATIVE THINKING YOU NEED TO SOLVE A MYSTERY.

Nod Nod

LET'S FIND OUT IF MR. FELS IS MISSING ANY GLUE.

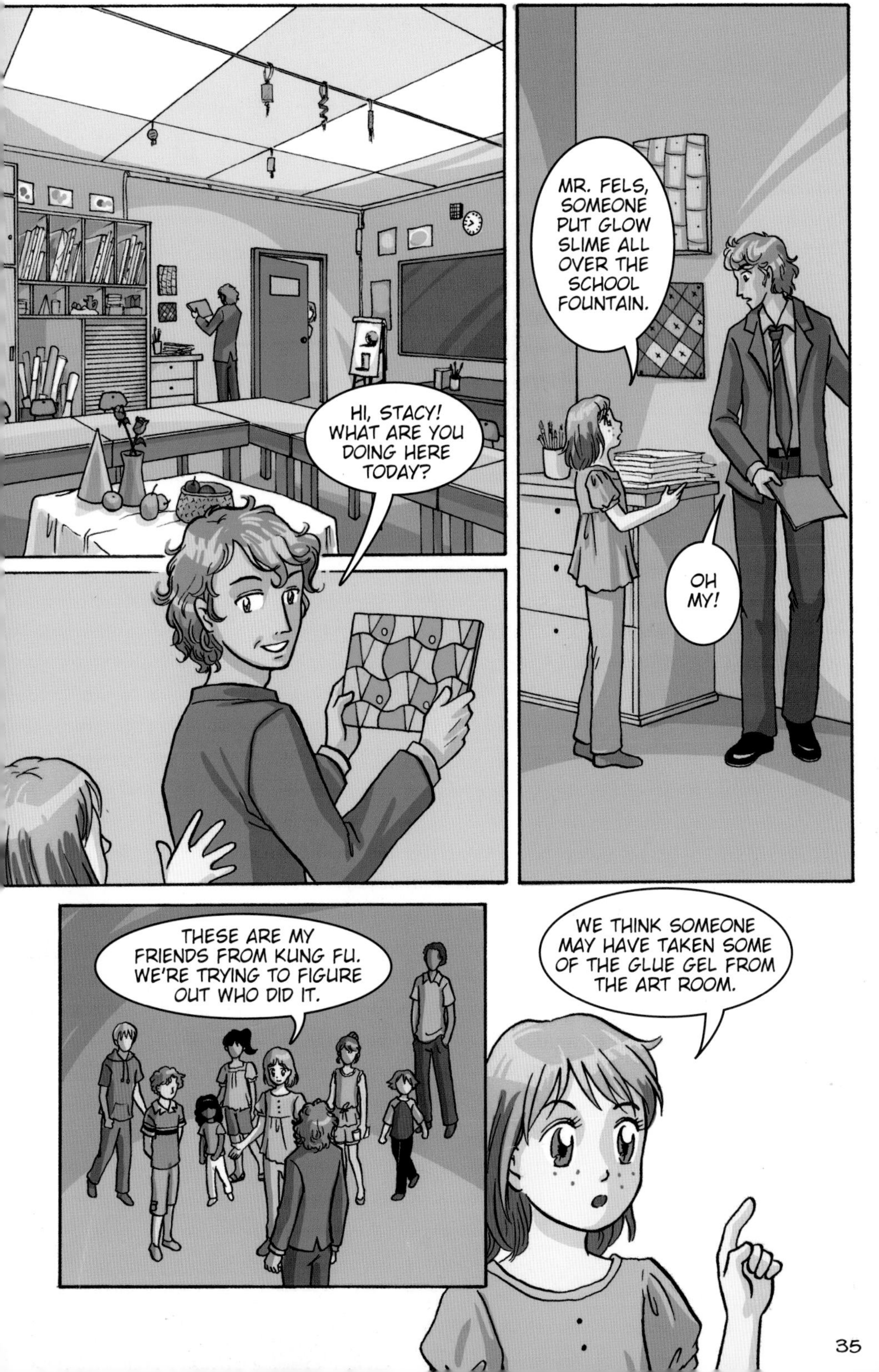
HI, STACY! WHAT ARE YOU DOING HERE TODAY?
MR. FELS, SOMEONE PUT GLOW SLIME ALL OVER THE SCHOOL FOUNTAIN.
OH MY!
THESE ARE MY FRIENDS FROM KUNG FU. WE'RE TRYING TO FIGURE OUT WHO DID IT.
WE THINK SOMEONE MAY HAVE TAKEN SOME OF THE GLUE GEL FROM THE ART ROOM.

WE HAVEN'T USED THE GLUE GEL FOR A WHILE.

Glue Gel

I *AM* MISSING SOME BOTTLES OF GLUE!

Inventory~

THIS SAYS THERE SHOULD BE 10 BOTTLES OF GLUE IN THE CABINET, BUT THERE ARE ONLY 2.

Inventory~
• Glitters - 15
• Brushes - 27
• Paints - 9
• Blue glue gel - 10
• rulers - 15
• paper - 6 boxes

Inventory~
• Glitters - 15
• Brushes - 27
• Paints - 9
• Blue glue gel - 10
• rulers - 15
• paper - 6 boxes
• canvas
• glow paint

10 − 2 = 8, SO THERE ARE 8 BOTTLES MISSING.

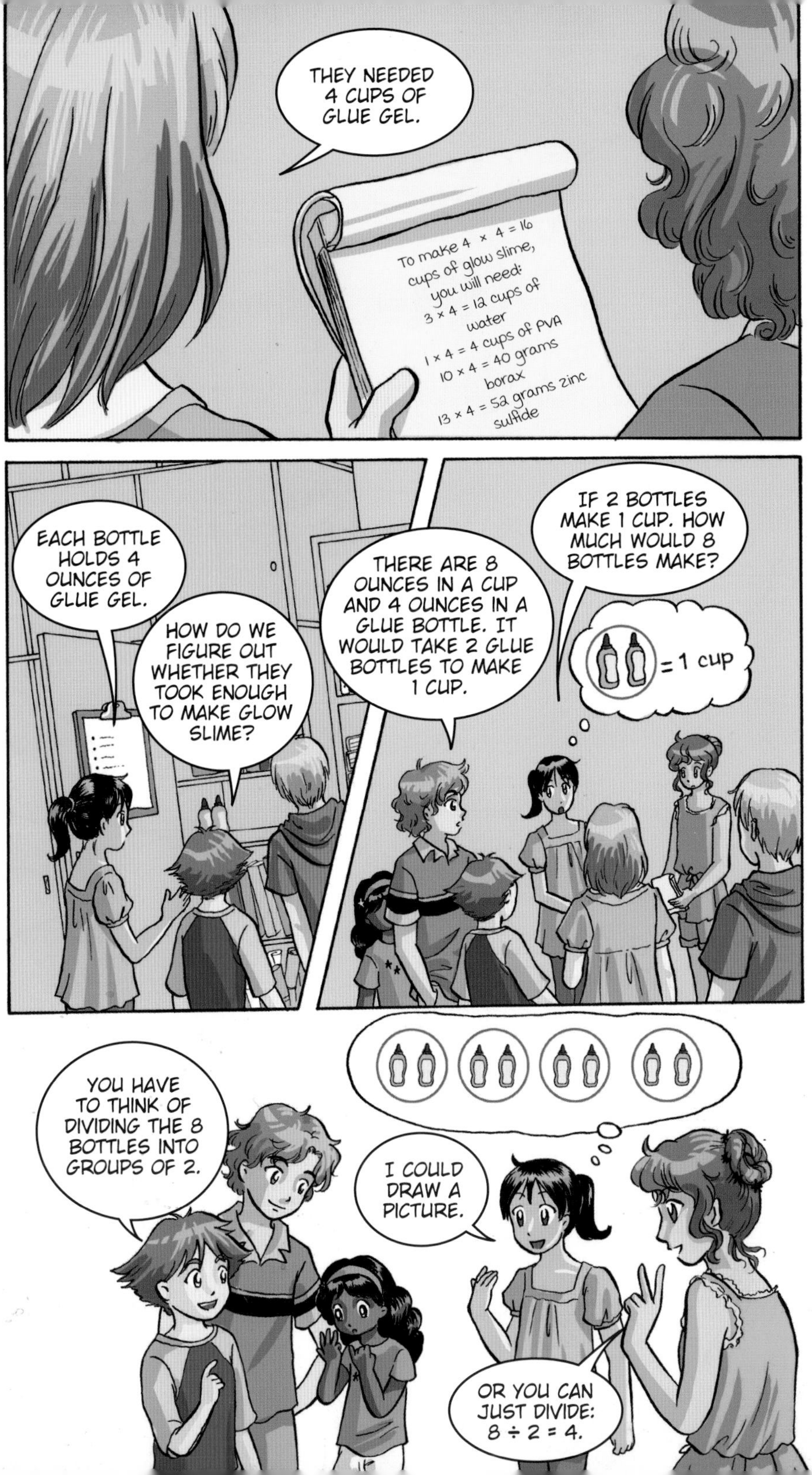
THEY NEEDED 4 CUPS OF GLUE GEL.
To make 4 × 4 = 16 cups of glow slime, you will need:
3 × 4 = 12 cups of water
1 × 4 = 4 cups of PVA
10 × 4 = 40 grams borax
13 × 4 = 52 grams zinc sulfide
EACH BOTTLE HOLDS 4 OUNCES OF GLUE GEL.
HOW DO WE FIGURE OUT WHETHER THEY TOOK ENOUGH TO MAKE GLOW SLIME?
THERE ARE 8 OUNCES IN A CUP AND 4 OUNCES IN A GLUE BOTTLE. IT WOULD TAKE 2 GLUE BOTTLES TO MAKE 1 CUP.
IF 2 BOTTLES MAKE 1 CUP. HOW MUCH WOULD 8 BOTTLES MAKE?
= 1 cup
YOU HAVE TO THINK OF DIVIDING THE 8 BOTTLES INTO GROUPS OF 2.
I COULD DRAW A PICTURE.
OR YOU CAN JUST DIVIDE: 8 ÷ 2 = 4.

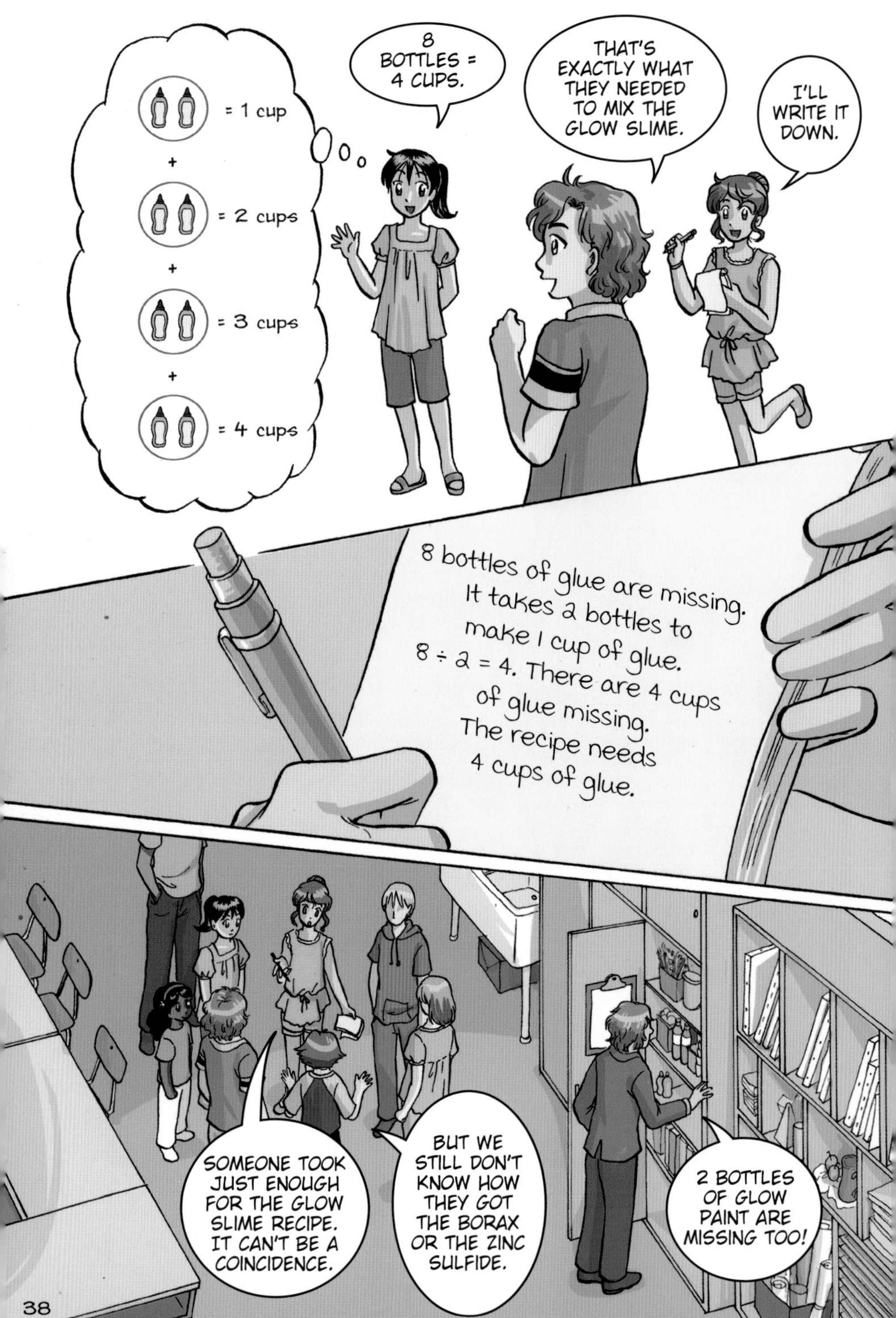
= 1 cup
+
= 2 cups
+
= 3 cups
+
= 4 cups
8 BOTTLES = 4 CUPS.
THAT'S EXACTLY WHAT THEY NEEDED TO MIX THE GLOW SLIME.
I'LL WRITE IT DOWN.
8 bottles of glue are missing. It takes 2 bottles to make 1 cup of glue. 8 ÷ 2 = 4. There are 4 cups of glue missing. The recipe needs 4 cups of glue.
SOMEONE TOOK JUST ENOUGH FOR THE GLOW SLIME RECIPE. IT CAN'T BE A COINCIDENCE.
BUT WE STILL DON'T KNOW HOW THEY GOT THE BORAX OR THE ZINC SULFIDE.
2 BOTTLES OF GLOW PAINT ARE MISSING TOO!

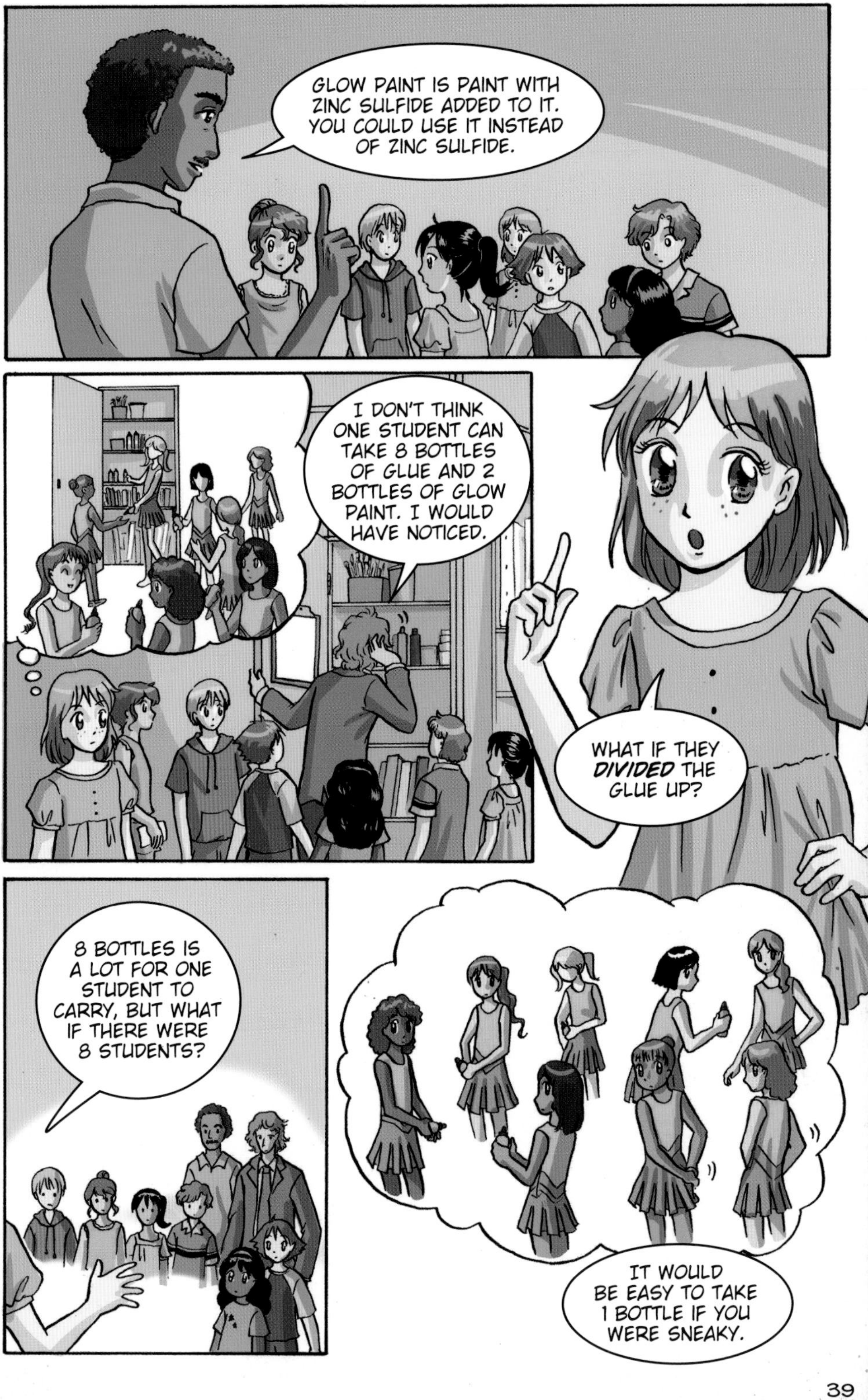
GLOW PAINT IS PAINT WITH ZINC SULFIDE ADDED TO IT. YOU COULD USE IT INSTEAD OF ZINC SULFIDE.
I DON'T THINK ONE STUDENT CAN TAKE 8 BOTTLES OF GLUE AND 2 BOTTLES OF GLOW PAINT. I WOULD HAVE NOTICED.
WHAT IF THEY *DIVIDED* THE GLUE UP?
8 BOTTLES IS A LOT FOR ONE STUDENT TO CARRY, BUT WHAT IF THERE WERE 8 STUDENTS?
IT WOULD BE EASY TO TAKE 1 BOTTLE IF YOU WERE SNEAKY.

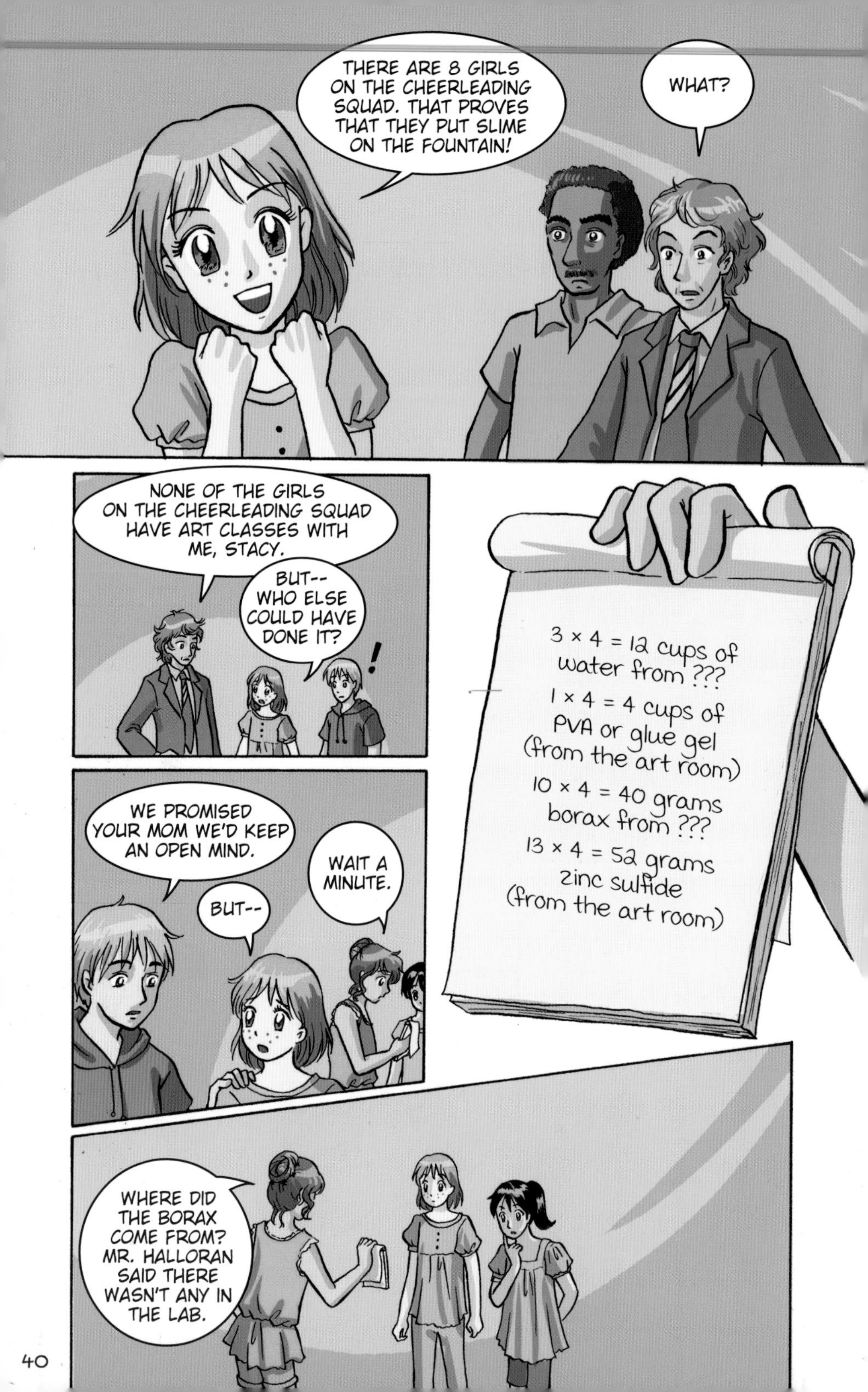
THERE ARE 8 GIRLS ON THE CHEERLEADING SQUAD. THAT PROVES THAT THEY PUT SLIME ON THE FOUNTAIN!
WHAT?
NONE OF THE GIRLS ON THE CHEERLEADING SQUAD HAVE ART CLASSES WITH ME, STACY.
BUT-- WHO ELSE COULD HAVE DONE IT?
!
WE PROMISED YOUR MOM WE'D KEEP AN OPEN MIND.
BUT--
WAIT A MINUTE.
3 × 4 = 12 cups of water from ???
1 × 4 = 4 cups of PVA or glue gel (from the art room)
10 × 4 = 40 grams borax from ???
13 × 4 = 52 grams zinc sulfide (from the art room)
WHERE DID THE BORAX COME FROM? MR. HALLORAN SAID THERE WASN'T ANY IN THE LAB.

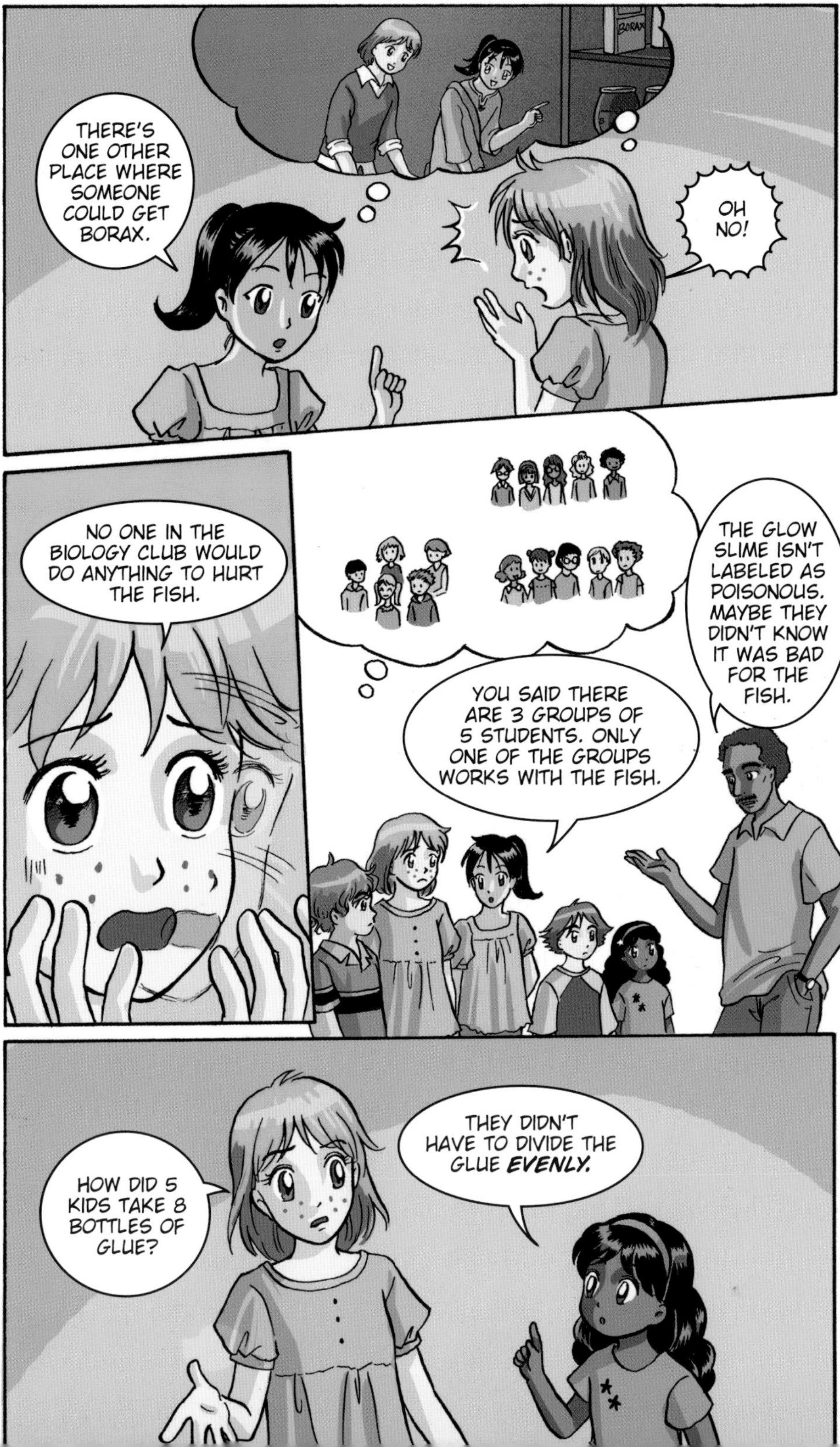
THERE'S ONE OTHER PLACE WHERE SOMEONE COULD GET BORAX.
BORAX
OH NO!
NO ONE IN THE BIOLOGY CLUB WOULD DO ANYTHING TO HURT THE FISH.
YOU SAID THERE ARE 3 GROUPS OF 5 STUDENTS. ONLY ONE OF THE GROUPS WORKS WITH THE FISH.
THE GLOW SLIME ISN'T LABELED AS POISONOUS. MAYBE THEY DIDN'T KNOW IT WAS BAD FOR THE FISH.
HOW DID 5 KIDS TAKE 8 BOTTLES OF GLUE?
THEY DIDN'T HAVE TO DIVIDE THE GLUE *EVENLY.*

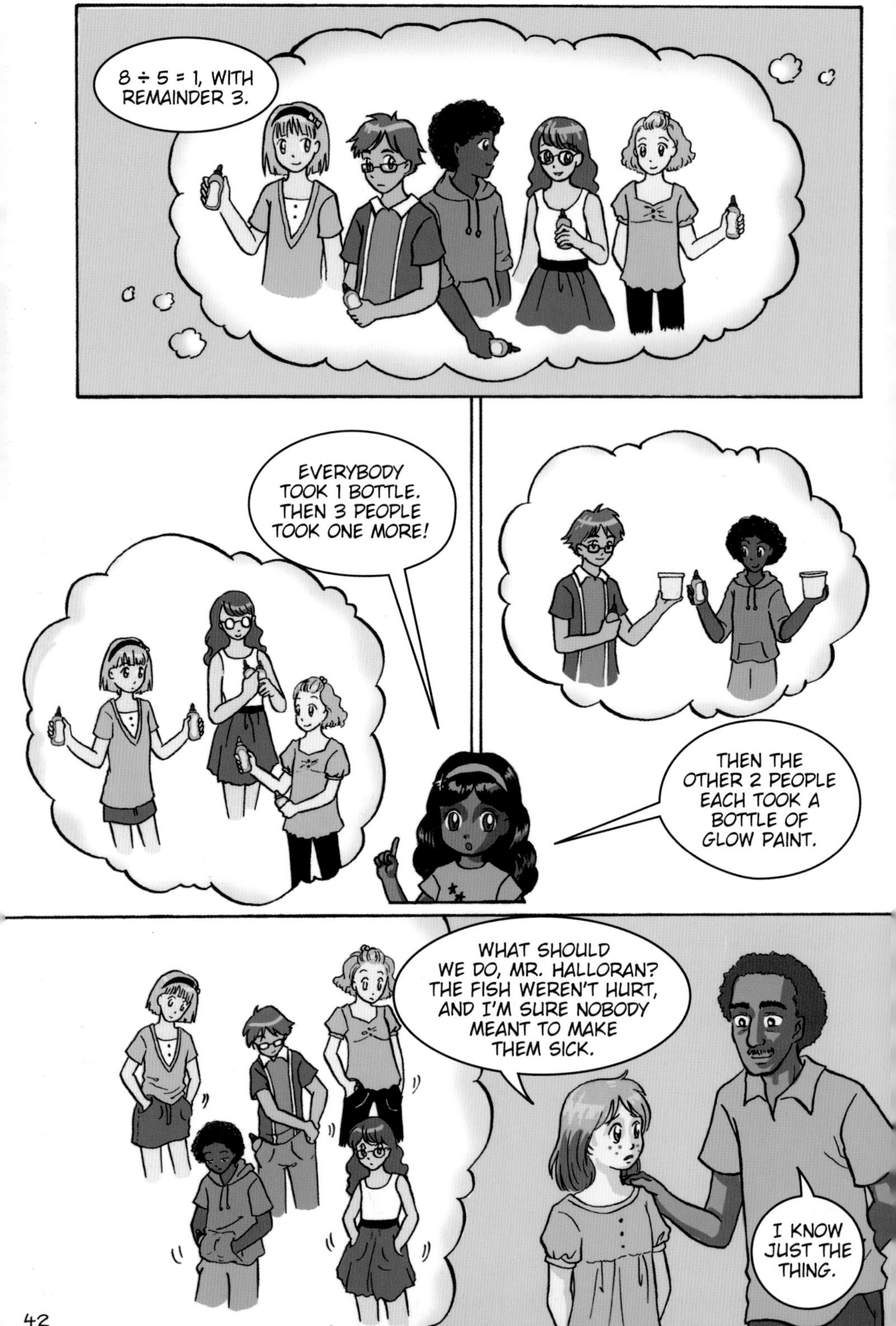
8 ÷ 5 = 1, WITH REMAINDER 3.
EVERYBODY TOOK 1 BOTTLE. THEN 3 PEOPLE TOOK ONE MORE!
THEN THE OTHER 2 PEOPLE EACH TOOK A BOTTLE OF GLOW PAINT.
WHAT SHOULD WE DO, MR. HALLORAN? THE FISH WEREN'T HURT, AND I'M SURE NOBODY MEANT TO MAKE THEM SICK.
I KNOW JUST THE THING.

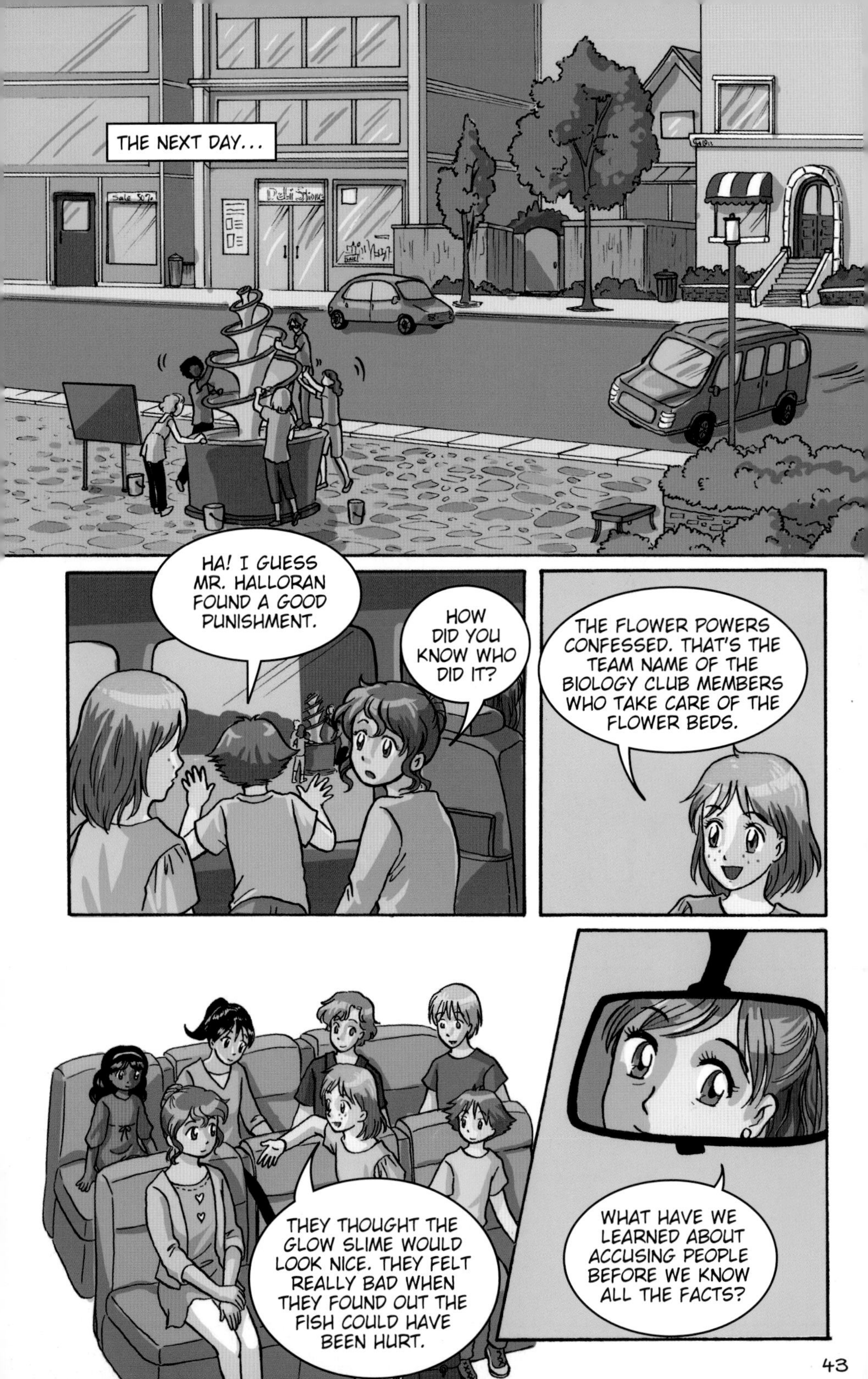
THE NEXT DAY...
HA! I GUESS MR. HALLORAN FOUND A GOOD PUNISHMENT.
HOW DID YOU KNOW WHO DID IT?
THE FLOWER POWERS CONFESSED. THAT'S THE TEAM NAME OF THE BIOLOGY CLUB MEMBERS WHO TAKE CARE OF THE FLOWER BEDS.
THEY THOUGHT THE GLOW SLIME WOULD LOOK NICE. THEY FELT REALLY BAD WHEN THEY FOUND OUT THE FISH COULD HAVE BEEN HURT.
WHAT HAVE WE LEARNED ABOUT ACCUSING PEOPLE BEFORE WE KNOW ALL THE FACTS?

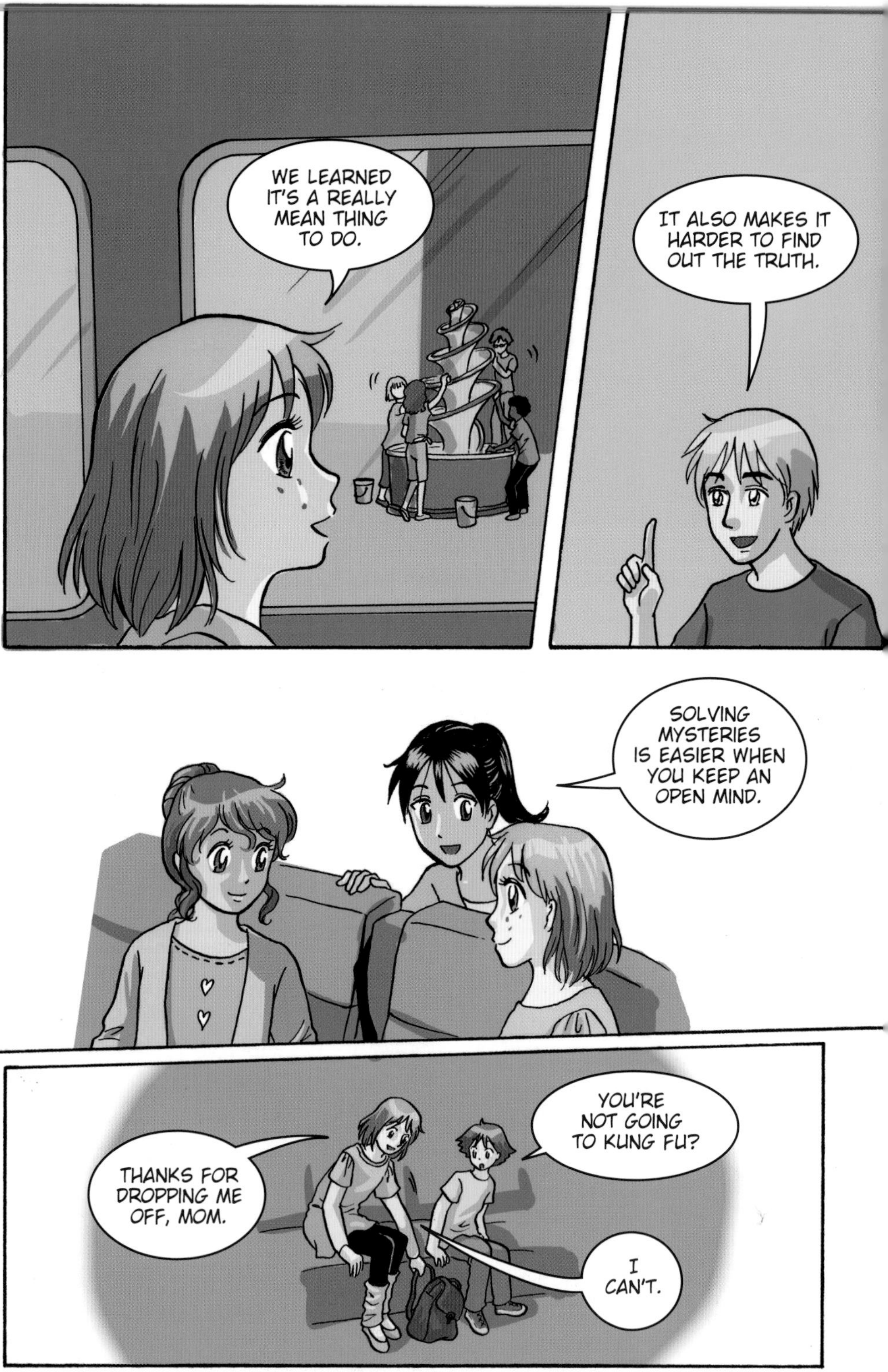
WE LEARNED IT'S A REALLY MEAN THING TO DO.
IT ALSO MAKES IT HARDER TO FIND OUT THE TRUTH.
SOLVING MYSTERIES IS EASIER WHEN YOU KEEP AN OPEN MIND.
THANKS FOR DROPPING ME OFF, MOM.
YOU'RE NOT GOING TO KUNG FU?
I CAN'T.

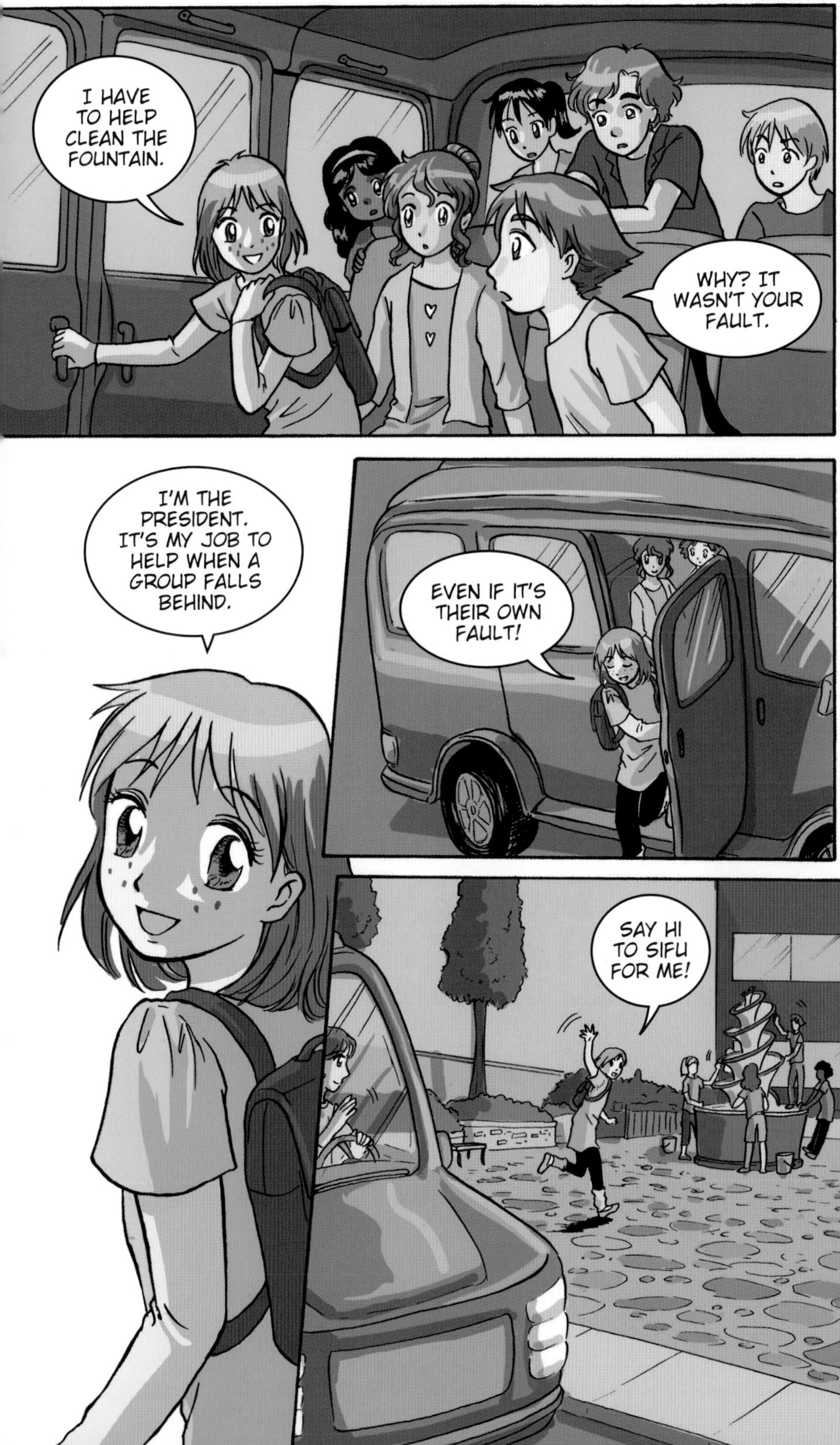
I HAVE TO HELP CLEAN THE FOUNTAIN.
WHY? IT WASN'T YOUR FAULT.
I'M THE PRESIDENT. IT'S MY JOB TO HELP WHEN A GROUP FALLS BEHIND.
EVEN IF IT'S THEIR OWN FAULT!
SAY HI TO SIFU FOR ME!

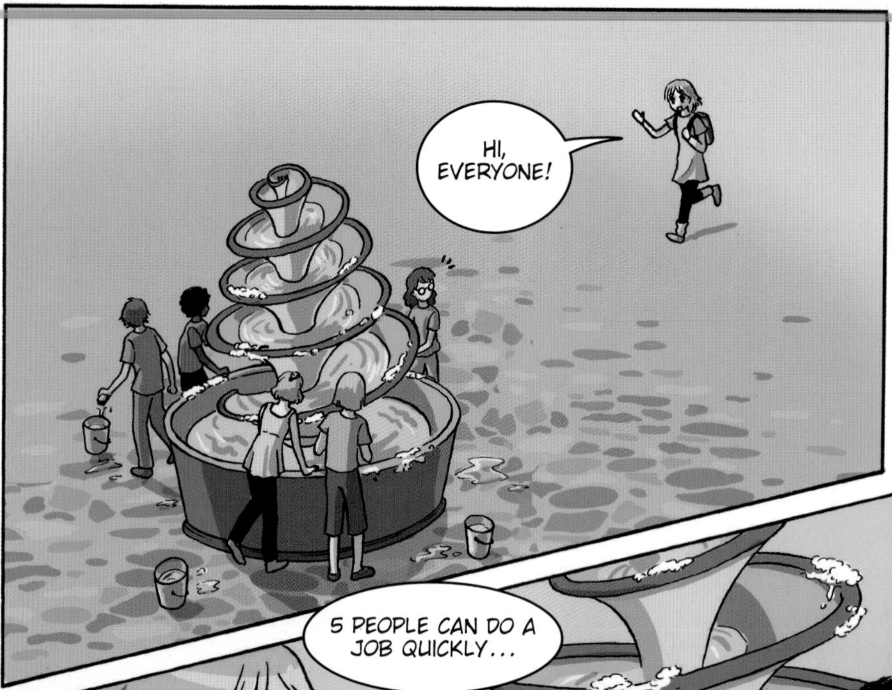
HI, EVERYONE!

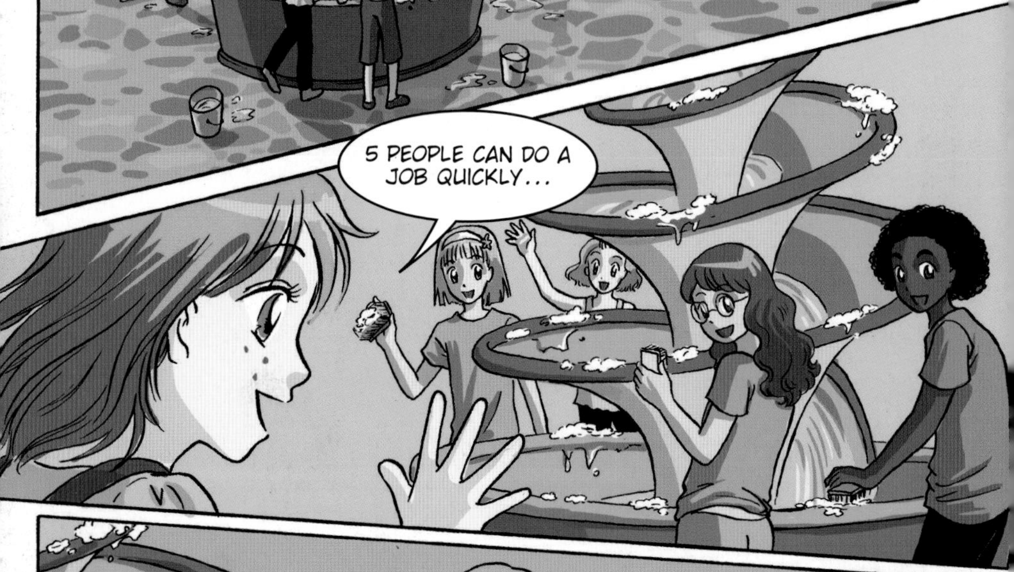
5 PEOPLE CAN DO A JOB QUICKLY...

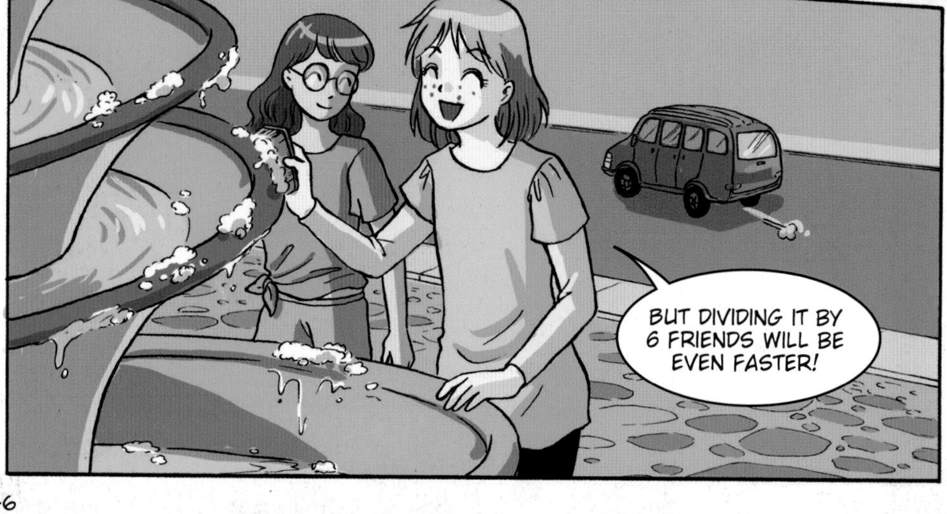
BUT DIVIDING IT BY 6 FRIENDS WILL BE EVEN FASTER!

The Author

Melinda Thielbar is a teacher who has written math courses for all ages, from kids to adults. In 2005 Melinda was awarded a VIGRE fellowship at North Carolina State University for PhD candidates "likely to make a strong contribution to education in mathematics." She lives in Raleigh, North Carolina, with her husband, author and video game programmer Richard Dansky, and their two cats.

Lydia Barriman is a is a teacher, doctoral candidate, and writer of math courses for all ages.

The Artists

Tintin Pantoja was born in Manila in the Philippines. She received a degree in Illustration and Cartooning from the School of Visual Arts (SVA) in New York City and was nominated for the Friends of Lulu "Best Newcomer" award. She was also a finalist in Tokyopop's Rising Stars of Manga 5.

Yali Lin was born in southern China and lived there for 11 years before moving to New York and graduating from SVA. She loves climbing trees, walking barefoot on grass, and chasing dragonflies. When not drawing, she teaches cartooning to teens.

Becky Grutzik received a degree in illustration from the University of Wisconsin-Stevens Point. In her free time, she and her husband, Matt Wendt, teach a class to kids on how to draw manga and superheroes.

Jenn Manley Lee was born in Clovis, New Mexico. After many travels, she settled in Portland, Oregon, where she works as a graphic designer. She keeps the home she shares with spouse Kip Manley and daughter Taran full of books, geeks, art, cats, and music.

Candice Chow studied animation at SVA and followed her interests through comics, manga, and graphic design. Her previous books include *Macbeth* (Wiley) with fellow SVA graduate **Eve Grandt**, who lives and works in Brooklyn, New York.

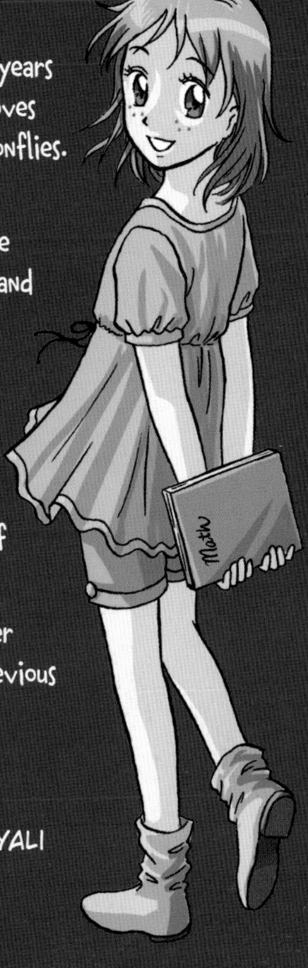
Math

STACY BY YALI

MANGA MATH MYSTERIES #7

When the science club creates a big "book bandit" sculpture in the public library, the librarians offer a prize to whoever can figure out how the sculpture fit in through the tiny window. The kids from Sifu Faiza's Kung Fu School know they can win, but it will take all of their geometry skills plus some unexpected cooperation to size up . . .

The Book Bandit

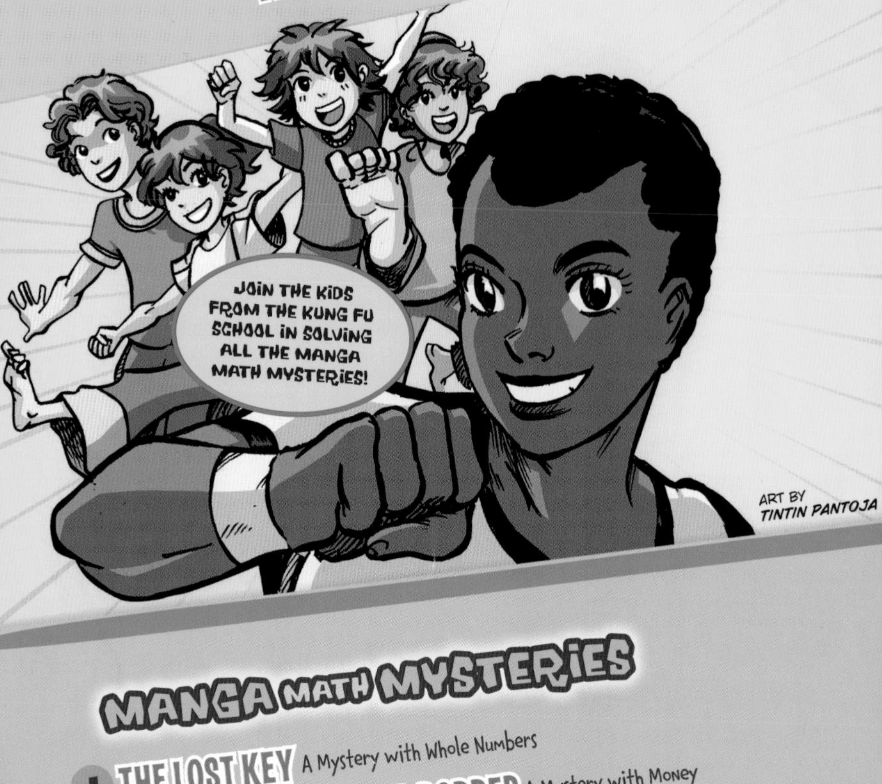
JOIN THE KIDS FROM THE KUNG FU SCHOOL IN SOLVING ALL THE MANGA MATH MYSTERIES!
ART BY TINTIN PANTOJA

MANGA MATH MYSTERIES

- #1 **THE LOST KEY** A Mystery with Whole Numbers
- #2 **THE HUNDRED-DOLLAR ROBBER** A Mystery with Money
- #3 **THE SECRET GHOST** A Mystery with Distance and Measurement
- #4 **THE KUNG FU PUZZLE** A Mystery with Time and Temperature
- #5 **THE ANCIENT FORMULA** A Mystery with Fractions
- #6 **THE FISHY FOUNTAIN** A Mystery with Multiplication and Division
- #7 **THE BOOK BANDIT** A Mystery with Geometry
- #8 **THE RUNAWAY PUPPY** A Mystery with Probability